A DISTANT BANNER

Henry Jones ought to have been good for something more than working as a scaffolder on a building site. He had a degree, the offer of a job, a girl-friend only too eager to settle down to Welsh respectability. Yet instead, he worked with O'Hara, violent and drunken; Davies, a drifter; Thomas, untrustworthy; Tommy Williams, universally disliked. All of them were in a state of running warfare with the foreman, a tough, hardworking Tynesider. When one of them is murdered, it is discovered that there has been considerable organized pilfering from the site. Henry is coerced by Inspector Morgan into unofficially working for the police.

A DISTANT BANNER

A DISTANT BANNER

by

Roy Lewis

Magna Large Print Books
Long Preston, North Yorkshire,
BD23 4ND, England.

British Library Cataloguing in Publication Data.

A catalogue record of this book is
available from the British Library

ISBN   978-0-7505-4487-0

First published in Great Britain 1976 by
William Collins Sons & Co. Ltd.

Cover illustration © vandervelden by arrangement with
iStock by Getty Images

The moral right of the author has been asserted

Published in Large Print 2017 by arrangement with
Roy Lewis

Magna Large Print is an imprint of Library Magna Books Ltd.

Printed and bound in Great Britain by
T.J. (International) Ltd., Cornwall, PL28 8RW

CHAPTER I

1

'Follow me, sonny.'

Henry did as he was told, even though the girder on which Geordie Banion was stepping seemed no more than two inches wide. The gulf that yawned ahead of them was perhaps eight feet across but it could have been a hundred yards the way Henry's heart spiralled down to his stomach. Banion strolled across the gap with a massive lack of concern that denied the existence of the eighty-feet drop to the ground, and the light breeze lifted the wide trouser bottoms he affected in a suit that had been fashionable fifteen years ago and was now relegated to a working blue serge, pin-striped, that marked him out from the rest of the crew. Only the foreman wore a suit, and Geordie Banion was foreman. That was why Henry did as he was told, and followed him.

The roofing contractors had already taken over across to their left. They were constructing a concrete floor and roof, building it from concrete joists and breeze blocks, but the crane that lifted the joists into place had been removed to another part of the site and the men were busy setting the breeze blocks into place beside the nine-inch brick wall that rose some twenty feet above the roof to lead to the next level. The roofers were desultory in their approach to the job and Banion hesitated, glancing at them uncertainly as though considering whipping them into line the way he did his own gang below, but then thought better of it. They were not his men, not his responsibility. He strode on across the completed part of the roof, his long ungainly stride bringing a smile to the faces of the men who watched him in his blue serge pin-striped suit. His ungainliness disappeared, however, when he reached the scaffolding and swarmed up it in quick, smooth movements. He moved quickly and confidently, like a spider whipping across to its victim, and when he reached the top and looked down at Henry, it was as though Henry was that victim.

'Come on, sonny. Get a move on.'

Henry gripped the first horizontal bar of the scaffolding and began to climb. It was neither difficult nor physically tiring as an operation, and yet with Geordie Banion watching him, grim-visaged, he found that his breath came short, his muscles trembled, he felt awkward and clumsy, and twice he missed his footing, slipped on the scaffolding and was forced to cling on with elbows and armpits while one gangling foot dangled down between the scaffolding poles.

'Don't be all day,' Banion grunted, turning away as Henry reached the top. He moved along the wall, stepped out on to a steel girder that would be used to support and underpin the concrete joists that were to be hoisted into place to make a roof again here, and headed for the knot of painters who were working on the gantry at the far end of the building. Henry stood on the wall, trembling slightly. The girder on which Banion stepped so confidently seemed narrower than ever and the movement of air, which was a light breeze far below, was a wind here, slight, but strong enough to disorient a man, cause him to make an error of judgement, pluck at his balance, move him, topple him. Eighty feet, a hundred feet... Henry did not look down.

Banion had stopped. He turned, looked back. They stared at each other. Banion was tall, perhaps six feet two inches in height. He wore a flat cap, brim pulled well forward, and the sun glinted on the greasy cloth. He had a dark, handsome, saturnine face, the features of an ascetic, a philosopher with eyes that read a man's soul and a mouth that never smiled. Henry felt that the man possessed almost superhuman intellectual capacities – his eyes held wisdom, his mouth the lines of experience, and his long, thin hands would have done many things, learned many crafts. And when Geordie Banion walked the high places it was difficult to realize he was merely a foreman on a building site, with contempt in his voice as he told a Sociology graduate that if he was bloody well scared to cross on the girders he shouldn't be working at Margam in the first place.

Maybe he had a point, at that. He wasn't the first person to have said it to Henry Jones during the last twelve weeks.

When the whistle blew, Henry was still forty feet above the ground. He came down painfully, slowly, carefully, scrambling down the scaffolding, crossing the completed roofs, picking his way through groups of men who unpacked their sandwiches and uncorked their flasks, some of them with their shirts off, sunning themselves, trying to pick up a tan so they had something other than mere money to show for their day's labour, and they didn't want to be dead fish white at the weekend at Porthcawl or Barry Island anyway. One or two of them grinned at Henry, nodded, but most of them either ignored him, or stared at him as though they had seen nothing like him in their lives before. Which was unfair. During the summer months more than a few students came to undertake casual labour at the steelworks, and on the building sites in particular. True, Henry Jones was different – he wasn't a student, he was a graduate in Sociology (with Politics, as his grandfather proudly added down in the Conservative Club every time he had the chance) – but there was still no reason why they should have been so obvious in their dislike of him. For Henry really believed that. They disliked him. He didn't fit into their pattern – he ate too delicately, he didn't pick his nose with grubby fingers or at all, for that matter, and he didn't indulge in the mindless, meaningless obscenities that flowed in their conversation, black and lumpy as the old Rhondda River. He was an unwelcome excrescence in the make-up of their working lives. They'd heard all about Sociology graduates at universities – trouble-makers they were, and there wasn't going to be any of that nonsense on this site. Unions yes, but piece-work bonuses were more important, and the day Henry Jones stepped out of line and tried to rabble-rouse they'd clobber him even before the management did.

Yet when Henry's feet touched the ground things changed somewhat.

Maybe it was simply because his feet *were* on the ground. But more likely, it was because there was one small group on the site who had come to accept him, and he was able to find a group identity with them – even if they were the misfits of the site.

They were already there at the foot of the concrete ramp when he finally made his way down from the building. They sat in a straight line, each of them facing the hazy summer sun, each masticating dry sandwiches that were curling at the edges, each taking an occasional sip from a stained personal flask cup, each saying nothing until the lunch break was half through, a ritual silence broken only by chewing, gurgling, an occasional hawking, a grunt, a shifting of position. Henry scrabbled under the ramp for his knapsack and took out his coffee flask, newer and brighter than the others in spite of his attempts to scratch it and stain it. He poured some coffee for himself, then opened his tommybox. It was an old one, and older than theirs – his grandfather's tommybox, the one he'd used in the pit. Cheese and pickle sandwiches, and some cold meat, and an apple. Henry leaned his back against the concrete ramp, easing himself into a position where his raw shoulders felt easier, and began to chew on a cheese and pickle sandwich. He closed his eyes...

'He's had you up the top, has he?'

Henry opened his eyes. It was Phil Irish who had

spoken. He was sitting hunched against the wall, a big, husky, easy-going man, shoulders that were barn-door broad with a smile to match, a man who got on easily with people but chose his friends and acquaintances and never allowed himself to *be* chosen.

'The foreman?' Henry asked.

'Aye. Had you up there, has he?'

Henry nodded. Phil Irish sipped his coffee noisily and stretched out his long legs.

'Bastard. Look at him up there. God playing God.'

Henry looked up. On the scaffolding, perched like a tall black monkey, was Geordie Banion. He was just standing there, one hand gripping the scaffold, splay feet braced, surveying the site.

'Like he owns the bloody place,' Phil Irish said. 'You know, I feel sometimes he can see every damn thing that happens on this site, knows what happens every minute, and you can't spit unless he knows it.'

'Can't see through concrete,' Jayo Davies said quietly. He said everything, and did everything, quietly. He was small in stature, mouse-like in appearance, undependable, sensitive, negligent, committed to avoiding work, intensely shy and uneasy at personal relationships. He was the scaffolder to whom Henry was mate, and he hardly ever spoke when they were alone together. Only in this small group did he relax somewhat, as though he could allow his own colourless personality to emerge within the anonymity of the group. 'Can't see through concrete,' he repeated, and Henry knew just what Jayo meant, and understood the

12

undertone of confident triumph in his voice. It was the only triumph in Jayo's life – his ability to beat the bosses, and win through to do nothing, idle an hour away, and get paid for doing it.

'Shouldn't have had you up there,' Phil Irish said in his amalgam of Irish brogue and Welsh flat vowel sounds. 'Over ninety feet and they're supposed to pay you a bonus – extra money, there is, for working at that height, danger money.'

'Only reason *I* do the job,' Tonto Thomas offered in agreement. 'Don't you go up there again, Henry. Tell bloody Geordie Banion to get stuffed. Tyneside bastard,' he added, making it sound as though it mattered.

And perhaps it did. For if they didn't fit, neither did Geordie Banion. They were a strange group altogether. Henry Jones, graduate in Sociology/ Politics, puzzling people who couldn't understand why he should choose to undertake manual labour of almost the lowest kind. Phil Irish, outwardly friendly and extrovert with those he felt inclined to charm but unwilling to speak to anyone he did not wish to; power, strength, rugged good looks and an unintelligent, single-minded application to life. Jayo Davies, shy, introverted, given to suddenly taking two days off work to sleep in the sand dunes at Port Talbot, and shambling back into work bleary-eyed and unshaven, without friends or enemies, a loner. And Eddie (Tonto) Thomas, who always said 'cawfee' and wore American leather boots with rubber soles and a wide leather belt, and who was reputed to play at gun-slinging weekends with the Nantyglo Alamo Club. He

13

sometimes sat making spitting sounds with his lips as though fighting out in his mind the battle at the OK Corral, where the slapping sounds of revolver and pistol shots were recreated through his stiff, committed lips. He needed the silences and the avoidance of friends to play out his gunfights, and he found them within this group.

And in a sense they fed off each other. Henry needed the group because they accepted him without question whereas suspicion stained the eyes of almost all others on the site. Phil and Jayo and Tonto asked no questions, for they lived their own private lives; they used the group, for they could not exist alone on the site. Other groups demanded participation or involvement; this one demanded nothing. Just people, near each other; a satisfaction of the gregarious need, but a rejection of commitment. And hovering over them, Geordie Banion – an outsider, a Northman, awkward and splay-footed on the ground but a cat among the girders, handsome and hawknosed, and grim and uncommunicative. Once or twice Phil Irish's eyes had said he hated Banion, but the hate had been lidded almost as soon as Henry caught a glimpse of it. There was more to it than the usual dislike of workman for foreman, just as it seemed to Henry there was more than mere *driving* in Geordie Banion's attitude towards the gang as a whole. Between Banion and the gang, and particularly between Banion and Phil Irish, there was an inexplicable enmity. Henry thought perhaps it was rooted in the fact that Banion was a Tynesider, and uncommitted to anything Welsh. Phil Irish, at least, had picked up mannerisms and phrases from

14

his years in Wales, but Banion remained defiantly Tyneside.

If Tonto Thomas disliked Geordie Banion, however, it was nothing to how he regarded another man on the site, and when Henry heard the groaning sound in Tonto Thomas's throat he looked up to see a little man walking across the broken ground towards them.

'Bloody hell,' Tonto Thomas said, and spat. There was a vicious gleam in his grey-flecked eyes. The little man drew closer with a peculiar rolling gait, like a sailor finding his sea-legs after months aboard ship, and he called out in a deep, confident tone, hail-fellow, well-met, knowing a welcome would lie for him with these good people.

'Hello, boys, how's it goin' then?'

Tonto Thomas spat again. 'Bugger off,' he said.

'That's what I like about you, Tonto, always jokin', isn't it?'

He stood in front of the small group, aggressively self-confident. He was not one of Geordie Banion's gang, but he spent a considerable amount of time in their company. Henry knew they all disliked him, and were repelled by him. Perhaps it was his manner, maybe it was that behind their dislike lay sympathy, or there was the possibility that deep rooted in each of them was an ancient fear, a primitive terror of the evil eye.

The little man had been born thirty years earlier, different from other people. As a child he had stood out from the rest at school, and now, as a man, he could not be avoided. He was just five feet tall and his arms were long, his shoulders powerful, his legs and body short and completely out of

15

proportion. But it was his head that produced the surprise, the *frisson,* in all who met him.

It was encephalitic in structure. Thomas Williams had a narrow jaw, a thin, laughing, humourless mouth, a square face with heavy ridged eyebrows and black eyes, and above was a wide, extensive forehead with bones that seemed almost to thrust their way out of his skull, protruding offensively, opening up under the sparse hair that provided a thin, inadequate covering for the blotchy skin.

A hundred years ago he might have been a monster that a village would have stoned and driven out of its midst; fifty years ago he might have become an idiot in an attic where he never saw the light of day, hidden by a shamed mother and an angry father; but it had been Thomas Williams's fortune and misfortune to be born into a childhood world that called him Tommy Bighead and a youthful world where adults took him and taught him and trained him and educated him and placed him in a competitive situation where he was not equipped to compete.

So Tommy Bighead had built his own equipment.

Another man in his situation would perhaps have crept away in a corner, sought darkness as a consolation, tried to hide his deformity from the eyes of normal people. The village community in which he lived would have preferred self-effacement; but he grew an emotional skin thick as oak bark, his voice grew louder, his walk became a swagger and he told the world what a great man he was, forced himself upon people as though to

16

demand their attention as he proclaimed his value, his intelligence, his intuitive skills, his *genius,* to the valley. And he *was* clever, Henry had heard enough people say that. He could even have gone to university, perhaps, if his mother hadn't repressed him in shame, and his father hadn't died inconsiderately in a pit accident, and if Tommy Bighead himself hadn't lacked the one quality that might have seen him through – application. For, clever though he might be, he lacked the ability to stick to anything. He moved from task to task, learning the rudiments of skills, never becoming skilled; picking up scraps of knowledge, never becoming knowledgeable. And his sharpness and his cleverness degenerated into a verbal, twisting, pyrotechnical conversation, where he could dazzle and blind and outshine the men with whom he lived. His jokes left them cold, or bit deep into their sensitivities. His tongue was a razor that scored their nerves, his malice the application of salt to the wounds he opened in their minds. Glinting, cutting, slashing, he was demonstrating his superiority in a world that saw itself his superior. It was Tommy Bighead's revenge on life, and life hated him for it.

He had spent the last ten years at various sites, inside the valleys and outside them. He came from the Rhondda, like Henry, but there was no firm in the valley that would employ him. He almost caused a strike at Treforest, some acid got spilled over a man's wrist at Cwmavon, and when Fred Bennet hanged himself in the old Mardy pit, down the lift shaft, Tommy Bighead got sacked as storeman. He took his malicious tongue to the building sites at Rhoose, and Llantwit Fardre, and several other places thereafter, and now he was in his seventh job at North Margam, above the steelworks.

But Tonto Thomas wished he was at the other end of the earth – or under it.

'We was peaceful sitting here until you came,' he said sourly, scowling up at the little man. 'Why don't you just push off?'

Tommy Bighead grinned, displaying large white teeth in a mirthless grimace. He held his arms wide, like a footballer appealing to an unmoved referee. 'What have I done already?' he pleaded in mock despair. 'Only just got here, I have, come to pay all due homage to the buckskin cavalier of Lower Nantyglo.'

Tonto Thomas hawked and spat and Tommy Bighead sidled a little nearer, winking slyly at Henry. 'Hey, Tonto, I heard old Rhys Morgan Rees was looking out for you at the weekend.'

'Whaffor?'

'He heard you had one up the spout, and thought they was talkin' about his daughter, and he lost a bit of sweat until he realized they meant you had a bullet up the barrel. Least, that's what I heard.'

Tonto Thomas's eyes seemed to have darkened; his long courtship with Glenys Rees was well known and he was touchy on the subject. He leaned forward now, drawing one American boot under him as though he was about to surge up to his feet and reach out for Tommy, but Phil Irish forestalled him.

'Stop your damned nonsense, Tommy. And

18

you, Tonto, don't let him needle you so much. Here, Tommy, you want some coffee?'

Tommy Bighead glanced across to Henry and then Tonto, still annoyed, but cooling, and there was a trace of disappointment in his voice when he spoke, as though he was reluctant to see Tonto subside so quickly. 'Aye, all right, then, Phil. Up to your old peacemakin' again then, is it? You know, Henry, our Phil is good at that.'

Phil Irish ignored the edge in Tommy's voice and threw away the coffee dregs from his mug before starting to pour some coffee from his flask into the mug. Tommy Bighead gave a little screech of protest.

'Hold on, boyo, don't put my coffee in that. Got my own cup, I have, don't want to catch any of them vicious Irish diseases, now do I? No desire to get Irish bogrot, like – you know where that strikes you, now don't you, Henry?' He leered in Henry's direction as Phil patiently waited for the little man to pass over his own mug. 'It don't strike your own home-raised Irishman, like; you'll understand, it's like haemophilia, Henry. Pass it on, but don't get caught yourself.'

He held out his mug and Phil began to pour out the coffee. His hand was quite steady as he said, 'You talk too much damned nonsense, Tommy, and one of these days your mouth will get you into trouble.'

'Ahh, don't believe that, boy. Too fast on my feet, I am, too nimble in the wits. Nothing to do with what I say, it's all in the speed with which I talk, see. Talk nonsense, yes, but talk it fast and people don't have time to grab at meanings; time they do, slow ones like you, it's too late. Meaning's gone; time to listen to something else.' He paused, grinned at Jayo Davies and sipped his coffee noisily. 'That's it, see, Jayo. Talk fast to an Irishman and you confuse him. That's why Phil here, he always watches the slow, easy programmes on television. Damn, he's still watchin' the old repeats of Muffin the Mule, you know that, Jayo? Someone ought to tell him, isn't that so?'

As unhappy as ever at being addressed directly, Jayo buried his face in his mug and mumbled. Tonto Thomas was less able to restrain his curiosity.

'Tell him what?' he demanded.

'That it's not illegal any more,' Tommy Bighead replied.

'What isn't?'

'Muffin the Mule!' Tommy shouted and began to laugh in the high, piercing falsetto that razored across the nerves like a fingernail against a blackboard. Tonto was looking blank until he saw the smile on Henry's face, then, still not appreciating the point, began to feel that he was being made the butt of Tommy Bighead's humour. 'One of these days...' he rumbled menacingly.

'One of these days you'll start work on time,' the cold voice said. All heads in the group turned to see the angular figure of Geordie Banion just ten feet away. He must have come down from the scaffolding at a remarkable speed, Henry thought.

'Ten minutes to go yet,' Tonto was saying petulantly.

'Not if you're due at the Abbey works, like you are. Truck's leaving in three minutes. Be on it. And

20

you, Jayo, and Jones, I want you up at the Craig-yr-Eos site end of the week or Monday at the latest, so get that scaffolding finished fast. All right?'

He turned, walked away abruptly without waiting for an answer, his stride awkward, hunching his lean form slightly as he walked, hands held stiffly at his side like a marionette. Henry marvelled again at the way the man changed when he was up above, light of foot, easy. Henry sighed.

'I'd better make a move,' he said. 'I've got to go back up with him first, Jayo, to clear the rubbish up there. Rate he climbs he'll be up there an hour before me if I don't go now.'

'You ought to be getting extra pay up there, over ninety feet,' Phil Irish warned him again.

'*Hell's flames!*' Tonto Thomas shouted, and scrambled to his feet, spitting. He threw his coffee aside, splashing it violently against the concrete ramp, then leaned forward angrily to inspect the wet patch trickling to the ground. 'What the hell is *that?*'

'Coffee sludge?' Tommy Bighead suggested, gently pouring his own coffee away in a slow, deliberate movement. 'Or a wet, squashed spider?'

Imperceptibly almost, he began to move away, keeping Phil Irish's legs between him and the reddening Tonto Thomas. The man was leaning forward, glaring at the black material he had spat out after sipping his coffee. Then the redness changed, a pallor coming under his skin. He raised his head, and turned towards Tommy Bighead.

'You dirty–'

Tommy Bighead's hands were up. 'Not me, what've I done? If you're so busy listening to your foreman, can I help it if some dirty great seagull–'

'You *put* that in my coffee,' Tonto Thomas bawled. 'I'll break your blasted neck, you stinking little–'

A distant whistle from the Abbey works cut across his anger. He grabbed up his haversack, thrust his flask and cup into it and swung it on his shoulder as Tommy Bighead, grinning mirthlessly, kept his distance. 'I'll get you again, you runt,' Tonto said, almost spitting out the words. 'We'll *settle* this!'

He turned, began to run away from the concrete ramp towards the site office where the truck stood, its engine coughing into life as the work force for the Abbey climbed over the tailboard. Henry watched as Tonto scrambled aboard, then he rose to his feet. It was time he made his way up the scaffolding again. Behind him, he heard Phil Irish say softly, 'You'll go too far, Tommy, one of these days.'

Tommy Bighead was chuckling. 'What you mean, Phil? You sayin' I put that muck in his coffee? Have to be one of the Magic Circle to do that.'

'You could have leaned over when we were looking at Geordie Banion.'

'Now why would I do that? And even if I did, *you* wouldn't let Tonto put his American boots on my face, would you, Phil?' There was a short silence, with no reply from Phil Irish, and then as Henry began to walk away he heard Tommy Bighead add, 'No, I know you wouldn't, Phil. You love me too much, isn't that it? I'm *good* to you, boyo, and you bloody well know it!'

2

Once a piece of scaffolding was finished and Jayo stepped back satisfied, raising his pale blue eyes up to admire briefly his handiwork, Geordie Banion would appear, timing Jayo to the minute. A perfunctory glance over the scaffold and then it would be pointing out a new erection to be undertaken. But no poles, no clips – they had to forage for them, scavenge the site for them. Relief for Henry's raw shoulders, boredom as Jayo played his game.

The poles and the clips lay scattered all over the site. They were left to lie where the last piece of scaffolding had been demolished, left to lie until they were needed for the next job. Friday afternoons a lorry came around sometimes to pick up the scattered equipment and pile it where the next week's major job would be done, and Young Beckie, the punchdrunk night-watchman, would keep an eye on it over the weekend. But by Tuesday afternoon, as the scaffolding crews busied themselves along the site, it would all become scattered again, and Jayo and Henry would begin their wanderings.

It was a time-consuming process. Jayo would slouch off with his hands buried deep in the pockets of his old flannel trousers, his worn toecaps scuffing at the dirt, occasionally taking a half-hearted kick at an old can. His head would be lowered between hunched shoulders, the grey stubbled chin rubbing slowly against his thick working-shirt collar, and he would be glancing from side to side in a quick birdlike manner, as though hoping that one day his prospecting would turn up something better and more exciting than mere scaffolding poles and clips.

Once under the shadow of the huge skeleton walls, and protected from Geordie Banion's eagle eye, his course became less erratic. Jayo had a nose for avoiding the materials he sought; his main objective was to see none and find none until he had spent as much time as he dared away from the scaffolding task. As Henry walked along behind him slowly, like an unhappy, uncomprehending puppy, Jayo led the way through to his favourite haunts among the rubble and dilapidation of sheds, half-destroyed buildings, Nissen huts, concrete bunkers, earthworks and half-finished foundations that made up the north end of the Margam building site. It was a place that never ceased to amaze Henry. It was nothing more and nothing less than a monument, in his eyes, to the economic disasters of the last twenty years. North Margam had opened up in 1950 as a brick-making concern, but a shortage of materials and orders had closed it within a year. Six months after the closure many of the buildings had been burned out by vandals, but the local politicians had announced that this was just as well for they intended opening up a brand new steel-rolling mill in place of the brickworks. The project then enjoyed almost ten years of planning blight until recession, strikes, inflation, union incalcitrance and employers' intransigence had caused abandonment of the whole idea.

Escalating costs had then faced a government uncommitted to saving a labour force that was intent on destroying itself, and the half-built rolling mill was finally dynamited.

All was not lost, in the opinion of the local politicians. There was talk of setting up a yarn-spinning factory; then a new industrial estate; then there were plans for light industry in North Margam, and after a sudden wave of enthusiasm in 1970 money had been poured in again to provide jobs and buildings.

An act of faith, the politicians said. Economic madness, the bankers remarked. It's money, and jobs, the men from the valleys said, and the pits were nearly all closed anyway.

But Jayo Davies said very little at all. He simply went on his perambulations – seemingly erratic, designed, as far as Henry could make out, to avoid the oversight of the foreman perched on the high girders, but taking in all the hiding-places that most suited Jayo, where it would be dark and secret and he could stand and be left alone. Henry guessed that Jayo saw the whole North Margam site in an entirely different light from him. For Jayo it was a haven, a place where he could come to work each day, earn enough money to be able to lose a few shifts and go back to dreaming among the Port Talbot sand dunes.

Henry's viewpoint was quite different. He appreciated that Jayo's path among the rubble had a curious consistency about it, dictated, he imagined, by the desire to hide and the availability of suitable places, but he was still surprised that Jayo could regard the place with such obvious affection. The after-effects of twenty years of incompetent planning had left the North Margam area more closely resembling a First World War battlefront than anything else Henry could imagine. But for Jayo it was a paradise. In his search for poles and clips he could wander into an old tin hut and crouch down in the evil-smelling darkness for twenty minutes at a time. He could crawl through drainpipes and make his entrance into a tomb-like cavern three feet underground, all that remained of fifteen-year-old boilers, lost under a pile of rubble. He could drop into concrete bunkers and lean against a girder, staring at the patch of blue sky above his head while around him water dripped and collected in little pools that glittered blackly in the faint light. Sometimes he took a smoke, but more often he did not. It was what Henry found so hard. For Jayo just stood there, saying nothing, making no attempt at social chatter, lost within himself, dreaming perhaps of the sand dunes just a mile away, of the cool grass on the valley hillside, or coal-streaked brooks that had been jet black before the pits closed and now seemed unwilling to regain their former state. He simply stood there, working hard at not working, and Henry shuffled, and coughed, and pretended to look for clips, even though scaffolding had never previously been erected in such places.

Geordie Banion knew about it but, as Jayo said, concrete was concrete and not even the hawk-eyed Northman could see through walls, or know where Jayo, mouse-like, had crept in.

It was only when Henry began to move around out of sheer boredom, poking around in the darkness, scuffling among timber and rubble and rubbish, that Jayo got uneasy, seemed to become aware of his surroundings. Once, Henry had begun to investigate some crates that were stacked in a dark corner of a bunker and Jayo had even pulled him away. It was as though he saw these hidden places as Pharaohs's tombs that hid him and succoured him and enabled him to win a small victory over his employers; and to poke among them, disturb them, was almost a sacrilege.

The day was always bright when Jayo and Henry emerged from these subterranean places, and Jayo would ask Henry the time – it was almost always a break of just twenty minutes – and then he would pick up his feet and weave through the rubble, collecting a few clips to make it seem as though his last twenty minutes scavenging had not been unprofitable, before he would come upon one of the scaffolding sites he would already have had pinpointed and would begin to demolish, preparatory to carrying the equipment to the place Banion had told him to raise another scaffold.

And then Henry's shoulders would begin to burn and he would ease the poles from the points of his shoulder along into the collarbone. His shoulders were sore and painful, and he gritted his teeth as he balanced three at a time, and he cursed all those other scaffolders who stole the light aluminium poles before he could lay his hands on them, and the long afternoons wore on and he said to himself that next week he could always pack it in, but he knew that at the end of *that* week he'd be there again, saying the same thing.

Everything else seemed pointless.

3

The train got in at the station just five minutes after seven. It was always a bit of a mad dash for Henry. They knocked off work at the site at five-thirty. The station bus left at five-thirty-five and the train left for the valley at five-fifty. It was a pleasant enough run after that, the diesel pulling surely away from the sprawl and smoke of Port Talbot until Henry could see a fading view of the sea, and then it was up into the hills, a long, winding green-sided track that wandered through narrow valleys and plunged into black tunnels and thundered out into the light again with a triumphant roar as it picked up the Swansea line, carved its way through the round-shouldered hills, sliced away in long swinging curves at the slopes and the rocks and the craggy, stream-strewn valleys towards the Rhondda. One last deep dive into a long black tunnel and they were out at the head of the valley, trundling past the silent pits and the smoking chimneys and the close, conspiratorial hum of the valley floor.

Henry's home lay with his grandparents, two miles from the station, through the village, past the Workmen's Institute and the Co-op and up the steep climb of the hill through the terraces to the last row, nestling under the greening slag of the fifty-year-old coaltip. It was a climb that had torn the breath out of generations of dust-lunged miners, and Granda himself came up from the club like an agonized grampus, whistling the breath out of his barrel chest, forcing it out to drag in another cramped half lungful under the coagulated dust on his tissues.

He wasn't home, of course, when Henry arrived. It was seven-thirty and the September sun had slipped below the mountain mist; Granda did his own bit of slipping at seven on the dot, in the direction of the Conservative Club down in the village, like all good committed Socialists. Nan was waiting for him, though, in the kitchen, already heaping Henry's plate with meat and cabbage and potatoes and gravy as though he was the hungry miner she had fed all those young years ago. Henry kissed her as he came into the kitchen. She barely reached his shoulder, a small, white-haired, defiantly Irish woman of seventy, with a wrinkled-nut face and sharp blue eyes, who had borne eight children and outlived them all, and now devoted herself to feeding her grandson, unquestioningly and with commitment. Talk and argument was for the men; she knew what she had to do. Valley women of her generation knew exactly what they had to do, and she counted herself a valley woman, in spite of her stubborn brogue, after more than fifty years.

'I'll go and have a wash first, Nan.'

'No need. Sit down and eat.'

Henry did as he was told. He wasn't hungry enough to attack the heaped plate with relish; physical labour left him too tired to eat heartily, but he knew better than to leave much on his plate. He toiled at it while his grandmother watched.

'On the scaffolding still, you are?'

'That's right.'

29

'With that Irish boyo?'

'Yes.'

'Don't you have much to do with the Irish. Bad lot, they are.'

It was her joke; she made it regularly, and Henry dutifully laughed and squeezed her arm as he rose from the table, promised her he'd have a cup of tea when he came down from the bathroom, and then made his way upstairs. The bath was new, the water deep and hot, and his body relaxed as the steam rose in the converted bedroom/bathroom and he tried to draw his thoughts together from the cobwebbed recesses of his mind.

'Henry?' A tapping on the door, his grand-mother's voice. 'Come on, how long you going to soak in there? Your tea's cold, and Brenda's come already.'

Brenda. The water was cool on his skin as he slid out of the dreams and stood up to dry him-self. Brenda was waiting.

They managed to get to the cinema in time for the main feature. It bored Henry and he dozed. When they came out, Brenda was querulous, but made no objection when he turned aside down the lane towards the old tennis club. The sport had not been stillborn in the village, but its childhood had never been lusty and it had died of atrophy within ten years. Youngsters from the council estate half a mile up the hill had broken down the fences, and it was easy enough for a young man to climb into the clubhouse. Henry climbed in and opened the door for Brenda. She came in slowly, and the dark-ness seemed warm when she was close to him, and they stood against the far wall, away from the window, and he felt the familiar places of her body.

There was petulance in her gesture when she thrust his hand away.

'Not tonight, Henry. I don't feel like it.'

'What's the matter?'

'I don't know,' she said, but he did. She had been like this for over two months.

'I'm fed up,' she said. Her skin gleamed palely in the faint light, and her reddish hair seemed black and thick against his cheek. 'It's not just the job, you know.'

'Isn't it?'

'It's the hours. You know what I mean,' she began to plead. 'I don't see much of you now. Damn, seems like I saw more of you when you were at university. But now, time you get back from work the evening's half gone. I got to call for you if we're to have any time together at all. Fridays is no good, because two out of three I have to work at the library; Saturdays, every other, I'm at work again. And even during the week, you're so tired and sore after that silly job you've taken ... but all in all, Henry, I just don't *understand*.'

'I've tried to explain. There's nothing else–'

'Rubbish,' she said quickly, flaring immediately. 'I got six O Levels and they got me a good job in the library. You got a degree–'

'But no uncle on the library committee.'

He regretted the words almost before they were out. It was not that he felt she would be angry at the implication behind the words – what he regretted was the inference she might draw from his remark, and when she seized on the words, reached the conclusion he dreaded, his heart sank.

'Is that what the trouble is, then?'

'Now, Brenda—'

She trampled all over his protest. Her eyes were bright, her mouth suddenly smiling, for she had seen his problem and knew the solution. 'You don't really know any councillors well enough, and you're too proud to make an approach yourself, that's what it is, Henry Jones. I can get around all that easy enough. Damn, Henry, there's several people I can have a word with, on the side, like, so there'll never be any suggestion that you—'

'*No!*' Brenda was startled by the vehemence in Henry's tone and she drew away slightly, a ridge of doubt appearing between her eyebrows, her body stiffening in a puzzled indignation. Henry continued, determined that she should not place him in a false position, or commit him to a course of action he did not favour. 'No, Brenda, I don't want you to talk to anyone about my getting a job. What I do with my life is my affair—'

'And nothing to do with me?' she interrupted angrily.

'Brenda, let me *finish*. Of course ... of course I'm concerned that ... well, we've known each other a long time and we're close—'

'*Close!*'

Her temper was really beginning to rise now; he could feel the indignation quivering in the muscles of her back. He held on to her tightly, determined to have his say, refusing to be sidetracked by the issues that he knew she was about to raise. 'I don't want you to go crawling around on my behalf, talking to people, *using* your contacts with them to enable me to get the kind of job *you* think I should have. The decision as to what I shall do with my life is *mine;* naturally, I have considerations to take into account, and you are one of them, but I cannot allow such considerations to dictate to me, or panic me into a course of conduct that may rankle with me for the rest of my life. I'll find my own job, Brenda, and at the moment the job at North Margam suits me. It's what I want to do; it's what I'm *going* to do, until I've worked out later–'

'Later!' Brenda was unable to contain her anger a moment longer. 'What are all these words you're using now, then? *Later* and *considerations* and *using* people and *crawling,* and as for saying we're *close...!* Look here, Henry Jones, I'm twenty-two years of age and you're even older! You've got no car, no money to spend, we have to skulk in holes like this to be together in private – it's like we were born thirty years before our time! People don't live like this now – things have changed, but you seem to want us to be rooted to the past. *Diawlch,* man, I've gone along with your old nonsense but I'm getting fed up. The way we are together we ought to be married, and it would be more comfortable at least in bed than on this creaky old floor! But since you graduated you've gone funny; no talk of marriage now, and this job is an excuse, it seems to me, to avoid me and all your responsibilities. Belittling everything, you are.'

'Brenda–' he began, fearing the tears. But there were none.

'I want to go home,' she said, and he had never heard her voice so cold.

33

At midnight, with three pints of beer inside his sagging belly, Granda always hit peak form. It was his custom to lean back in the old wooden armchair, put one boot up where the blackleaded hob used to be and where an electric fire now dispensed cheerless heat, and talk about the old days. Black Friday when the General Strike collapsed and the miners were sold down the river; older brother Edward getting a bullet in his eye at Mons; the day Winston Churchill sent the soldiers to Tonypandy; pit falls, broken wrists, a drunken Irish doctor who hanged himself before cirrhosis could get him, and politics, local and national.

'Now take you, Henry,' the old man was saying. 'Got to admit, when you took up this Sociology thing, I was disappointed. Your father should have been a teacher, but there was no jobs and you was on the way; you should have been a teacher, it's what I planned for you when you came to us. Disappointed, I was, when you said you was going to read Sociology. Rubbish. But then, you did some politics as well and I thought it was all right, boy, you'd make out yet. But you never talk, Henry, you never *talk* politics.'

Henry had heard the conversation for more than two years. The old man would sit there night after night, broad, barrel-chested, his frizzled grey hair cut short and his blue-scarred forehead gleaming in the light as he fixed Henry with an earnest glance and insisted the question be answered– 'Why don't you talk politics?'

Henry wasn't interested in politics. It was part of his degree, a minor study area, not politics in

Granda's sense of the word. Granda saw politics as only one thing: the battle between the workers and the employers. And he didn't see the discrepancy that lay between such a viewpoint of class commitment and his other plaint against Henry– 'Why are you working at Margam?'

Tonight, like other nights, he thumped the table with a gnarled fist.

'You got *brains*, boy, and you ought to be usin' them! Maybe you got them from me, for I've read a few books in my time, and your father, well, he was a *voracious* reader, you'd think books was spinach with him and he wanted muscles like Tarzan, if you know what I mean. But the time took away my opportunity, and the war took away your father's, and it's in you the hopes of both of us rest. Can't you see that? All right, maybe you don't want to be a teacher. Can't understand that, teachers got *status* in the valley, you know, but that's all right, I can accept it. If it's money you want to make you ought to be a solicitor like old Gwilym Evans, rolling in it, he is, but you don't seem to think much of money. But a good *clean* job is what you want, boy, one you can hold your head up in, and one that'll help you make your way so you can use your Politics degree, get a seat on the council, make the Party sit up and then, well, safe seats around here in plenty in spite of those soft Welsh Nationalists–'

'Granda, you don't understand, how can I explain–'

'Now, Trehafod, there's a job comin' up there: I was talking to Tucker down the club tonight. Playing billiards, he was, and he happened to say

35

that the banks are takin' more graduates these days. You'd be a manager before you look around. Good job, you know, and maybe step out of it, professional career behind you and all that, and who knows what lies ahead?'

'I don't really think–'

The old man ignored him. It was as if he was dreaming, looking to lost opportunities that were his now, through his grandson, a chance to do for himself what he had missed, to obtain vicariously those chances in life that had never come his way. 'I could have a word with Dai Morgan; he married Jack Fletcher's aunt, you know, that old woman who used to live in Tynewydd and took up with that insurance agent; Dai is in well with Jenkins Post and he owes me a favour from way back. Now I can have a chat with them–'

'I don't want to work in a bank, Granda.'

The old eyes cleared as though cataracts of forgetfulness had been lifted from them. He stared at Henry as though he had never seen him before.

'You can't *want* to work at Margam, boy.'

'*You* worked down the pits for forty years. What's so bad about Margam?'

'But you've had a *chance;* dammit, I didn't, and your father didn't, and...' He was shaking his grizzled head in the same angry exasperation he had shown for the last four months. 'How can I explain to you, Henry? You're *drifting,* boy. I learned early, as a young man, you got to have an aim in life. You got to know where you want to go. It's like having a point to aim for, a flag far away, a distant banner to strive for...'

And with you, Henry thought sadly, the point at

36

which you aimed had been such a simple one. Chairman of the Co-operative Stores Committee. Status, importance, a leg of lamb smuggled into a sack of flour at Christmas, a pound of raisins around the back door once a week. And you made it. After twenty years of political activity, working on the library committee in the Workmen's Institute, canvassing for the local candidates, joining political rallies and supporting the Cause, you made it. Chairman of the Co-operative Stores Committee. Licensed, small-scale corruption, justified by the argument that you had worked for years for the good of the valley miners, in many ways, so many, many ways.

'...but you don't seem to have any aim, Henry. So where's it going to end; where are *you* going to end, boy?' It was a question Henry could never answer.

4

'What big shoulders you got, said Mr Wolf.'

Henry nodded, and huddled in the corner of the carriage as Tommy Bighead clambered in behind him, his long arms pulling his misshapen body forward in a shambling leap. He threw his knapsack on the roof-rack and sat down heavily beside Henry.

'Bit sharp this morning, like the actress said—'
'It is.'

Henry knew that he was doomed to an hour's chatter. He huddled deeper into his coat with the collar turned up and looked out of the window bleakly. Tommy Bighead didn't mind.

'When you joined us at Margam you looked a bit weedy, you know? Tall, aye, and strong enough, but a bit *weedy*. Timmy Hendy reckoned you wouldn't last the week, bein' a Sociology graduate and all. I wasn't so sure. But you didn't only stay, did you? Put on *muscles* as well.' He chuckled. 'Come for the nobility of labour, you have, and get muscles thrown in. Great, init?'

Tommy Bighead knew it was padding. The first few days that Henry had worked at Margam he had found the scaffolding poles heavy, but manageable, once he learned how to balance them properly. But the rawness of his skin was something else, and he could not cope with it. It had almost made him leave the job, but he had stuck to it out of sheer determination, because Granda and all the workmen at Margam expected him to pack it in within the week. And come Saturday Granda had taken his old jacket and sewn strips of thick cloth into the shoulders. They gave some relief, not much, but a little. The trouble was that Granda's inexpert needlework had given Henry the appearance of an American quarterback. Tommy Bighead had been swift to seize the point and make capital of it. For two days Henry had endured the jokes, but it was only when they were returning to the Rhondda on the train that Tommy Bighead had stopped. Tired of the constant sniping nonsense Henry had turned on him.

'Just what is the matter with you, Tommy? Are you too thick to know when a joke is outworn, or is it just that the joke is a cover for something else?'

The little man's eyes had lit up with malice. 'Can't take a joke, is it, Henry? Big lad like you, cosseted in university, begrudging a bit of fun for someone like me.'

'Like you? What are you like, Tommy?'

'Catch as catch can; guess as guess can.'

'Oh, I can guess all right,' Henry had said grimly.

And Henry had guessed. He'd dredged out of his psychology lectures all the old half-forgotten rubbish he could remember; he'd talked about looking for identity, about the desire to conform; he'd mentioned how people were only looking for love when they acted in a deviant fashion; he spoke of groups and peers and the value-judgements people make of each other and their rivals. And out of all the mish-mash something bit home; at the end of twenty minutes Tommy Bighead didn't want to talk. Henry had dried up, aware of the suppressed agony in Tommy Bighead's face. And at that point he began to pity Tommy Bighead – not in the way others pitied him, with a pity that turned to dislike when they felt the barb of his tongue and the malice of his practical jokes. It was a pity for the man inside the misshapen body, a sadness for his soul. And Tommy saw it in Henry's eyes, recognized it, and was afraid.

He stayed away from Henry for three days, avoided him on the station and on site. When he finally came breezing around again, nothing seemed to have changed outwardly, but Henry knew otherwise. For Tommy Bighead made few gibes at Henry Jones; the few he made were, in addition, lacking in the malice he displayed else-where. But that malice directed to others on the site became even more bitter. His practical joking became almost frenetic on occasions, as though he were trying to show Henry he was wrong in whatever he had said. Henry's pseudo-psychological discourse had deeply impressed Tommy Bighead and the misshapen man had no desire to attack Henry Jones. He was too formidable an opponent. The others – big, thick Phil Irish, vulnerable Jayo Davies, petty, vicious Tonto Thomas – they might offer him physical violence when roused but he could deal with that, it was part of the game anyway. Offer violence to a misshapen little man and who was the loser? But words were another matter; Tommy felt Henry could expose him, had the verbal agility and intellectual power to probe inside him, and it was something he could not use and control. So Henry was dangerous.

And, paradoxically, as near to a friend as Tommy Bighead could manage.

And this morning, on the train, Tommy was in a confiding mood. There were just the two of them in the carriage, and each time the train stopped Tommy pushed his face against the window so that would-be boarders looked elsewhere for seats. So they were alone together, and Henry heard of Tommy's exploits at Margam and Llanwern, Treforest and Llandaff, at pitheads and steelworks and offices from Cardiff to Swansea. It was a sad, dreary, repetitive, malice-ridden tale, and yet Tommy Bighead related the incidents with gleeful relish. There were filthy stories in which human excrement played a central part, there were violent incidents where a man could have been killed, there were spiteful, mean and unpleasant tales where the innate despair of Tommy Bighead as a man stood revealed for Henry. For if by telling his tales Tommy Bighead hoped to cloak his true self with a veneer of confident action – a man in a man's world – he failed. He merely exposed himself more than ever to Henry, who, untouched of late by Tommy's personal malice, was able to view dispassionately the little man by his side. And particularly so, now that he had the key.

'Puck,' he broke in after a while.

'What's that?' Tommy Bighead said sharply.

'It's how you see yourself,' Henry said. 'Puck. Small, clever, frightening country folk out of their wits, malicious and wicked with your sense of fun, but lovable.'

Tommy Bighead had eyes that could blank out in a disturbing way, as though he were turning his glance inward, and it was one of those moments now. 'Is that how *you* see me, Henry?'

'I didn't say that. I think it's how you see yourself. Or *want* to see yourself.'

And so it was. Tommy was silent the rest of the way to Margam. When they left the station he made sure he sat away from Henry at the back of the bus. Henry had the feeling that Tommy Bighead was afraid of him as he was afraid of no other man on earth.

It was a bad day.

It had started badly, with Henry having to rush from home without breakfast, since he'd risen late in spite of Nan's call. It continued badly with the trip with Tommy Bighead, because Henry was left with an uneasy feeling after the conversation in the

41

train, as though he had been kicking a dog that refused to yelp.

And then there was Morris Weasel.

Daniel Morris worked in the site office. His duties included, as far as Henry could make out, the supervision of time-sheets and clocking in, the control of materials and organization of labour, the servicing of the Abbey works and the co-ordination of foremen's activities. He was not a clerk of works – that was a man called O'Connor, who was rarely seen on site – but he deputized in most of the tasks that a clerk of works would normally undertake. He was an elusive man; early mornings and late afternoons he could be caught in his office, and he took his lunch there too, but the rest of the day seemed to be spent in an eternal perambulation around the site, writing in a little black book he carried in the dilapidated waistcoat he wore under his black jacket.

He was small, quick-tongued and quicker-tempered, dark, shifty-eyed, and always seemed to be in need of a shave. He had a disconcerting habit, when writing in his little black book, of opening his mouth like a goldfish, making a popping sound as he did so. To him, it seemed, it served the same nervous purpose as pulling an ear or scratching a nose served others, but it had led to his Christian name being discarded by workmen on the site in favour of the sobriquet they had given him.

But this morning if anything was popping it was the atmosphere at the office just inside the site gate. Phil Irish was there, with Jayo Davies unhappy in the background, Tonto Thomas was stamping up and down in his American boots, and Tommy Bighead was waving an angry fist in front of Morris Weasel's sharp nose.

'What the hell do you expect *me* to do about it?' Morris Weasel was shouting. 'Come on, boys, you know this is none of my doing! All I got to go on is the reports that I get in from the foremen, and I just got to go by what your foreman puts down. According to his time-sheets for overtime, you lot put in eight hours last week, not twelve. Now that's what I go by. You signed the bloody things, after all!'

'But they was *blank* when we signed them,' Tonto Thomas almost screamed. 'You know the bloody system! Geordie Banion brings the papers around like the other foremen do, and we sign them beginning of the shift, when we agree how long we're goin' to stay on. He writes in the figures–'

'Well, he wrote in *these* figures,' Morris Weasel insisted, 'and that's what I go by. Hell, it's not as though you lot's short of a few bob–'

'The hell with that,' Phil Irish almost snarled at him. 'I'm always short–'

'That's because you're always strappin' like the stupid Irishman you are,' Morris Weasel shouted. There was a quick silence and Morris stood staring at Phil Irish as the big man glared at him. Henry could not be sure that Phil was angry about the remark concerning his 'strapping' – taking advances on his pay – or was annoyed at the reference to being Irish. But his anger was real – and then suddenly there was something else in the air, as the anger evaporated, the excitement cooled. Tonto Thomas seemed to become aware for the first time that their shouting match was drawing attention, that a group of men were still waiting to come in through the gate. Jayo Davies was already moving away, shambling sideways as though demonstrating, crab-like, that he was not really of this group. And strangely enough the verbal violence that had lain between Morris Weasel and Phil Irish, and had been on the point of changing to a physical violence, was dissipating as the two men eyed each other. Henry felt they were reaching an understanding, grabbing for a piece of knowledge they both possessed and had half forgotten. It was Tommy Bighead who broke the spell.

'Geordie Banion is the bastard.'

The group and the quarrel broke up abruptly, and Phil Irish walked away on stiff legs, anger smouldering in his eyes. But when Henry looked back over his shoulder, Tommy Bighead was still at the gate. The last of the men were on site, clocking in had ended, but Tommy Bighead was still there, talking to Morris Weasel. There was nothing friendly in their attitudes. Henry was forcibly reminded of two bantam cocks, ready to claw each other to death.

The day stayed evil in taste.

Geordie Banion came down to them at the coffee break, and Phil Irish raised the matter immediately. He sat sprawled with his back against the concrete ramp as usual, and when the tall, splay-footed Tynesider came striding across the site towards them he put down his coffee mug and clenched his fist.

'*Banion!*'

The foreman's narrow eyes seemed to become slits as he heard his name. His stride did not change; he strode forward and stood just two feet from Phil Irish's contemptuous form.

'You want to speak to me, O'Hara?'

Henry's eyes widened. It was the first time he'd heard Phil Irish's surname; oddly enough, he'd always assumed his surname *was* Irish.

'That's right. I want to know what the hell you're playin' at.'

'About what?'

'Time-sheets.'

'You got a complaint, O'Hara?'

'Sure as hell I have.' Phil Irish scrambled to his feet. His handsome, rugged features were blotchy with a subdued anger and a harsh edge crept into his tone. 'You made a hell of a mess of our overtime sheets. Deliberately.'

'A mess, no. Deliberately, yes.' Banion's eyes were glittering dangerously; he was neither cowed nor alarmed by Phil Irish's threatening demeanour. 'You'll get paid today for the work you did.'

'I strapped thirty quid last Tuesday,' Phil Irish said, 'and I was counting on a full wage packet this week with the overtime. But you counted up only eight hours. I wanna–'

'Let's get this straight, O'Hara. If you don't like working on this site, get off it. But while you're still here you'll do it by the book. All right, you strapped thirty quid. That's your affair – if you want an advance on your wages every week that's up to you. But all you damn Irish are the same. You strap for half your wages, then complain when you have to make it up. The alternative is overtime

45

– *or something else.*' He paused, and the silence grew around them, heavy and dangerous. 'But if it's overtime, you get paid for what you do. You, and Davies, and that bloody cowboy there, you all agreed to do a full period of overtime four days last week. But you never *finished* one period.'

'You can't know that,' Tonto Thomas said angrily. 'You knocked off, damn it–'

'My job gets done whether I'm on site or not,' Banion snapped, without looking at Thomas. His eyes remained fixed on Phil Irish. 'And my job is to sign overtime sheets to say you did the work. You didn't do it; you didn't put in the time.'

'The materials–' Tonto Thomas began to complain.

'It was nothing to do with materials,' Banion interrupted. '*Was it,* O'Hara?'

Phil Irish was a long time replying. His forehead was furrowed, as though he was trying to puzzle something out, but the anger had retreated in his eyes, sinking, to be replaced with confusion as conflicting images clouded his brain. He shook his head slowly. 'No ... it wasn't anything to do with materials.'

Geordie Banion's hawk-like features showed no sign of relaxation but some of the tension was gone from his whipcord body. He stuck his hands in his pockets and looked around at the silent group. 'You get paid for what you *do,* boys, and no more. Remember that. Now, Jayo!'

Jayo Davies came out from behind his sandwich. His eyes managed not to meet Banion's and perhaps it was that failure which caused contempt to enter the foreman's voice. 'I want you and your

46

mate to get the lorry down to the Craig-yr-Eos site. This afternoon. The painters are screamin' down there. So move yourselves. Now.'

They moved. Phil Irish did not. He stood there, staring at Geordie Banion, and the vague puzzlement was still in his eyes.

Craig-yr-Eos was a grand place to be on a sunny afternoon. From the top of the hill there was a view right out to sea and the grass was green and springy, larks sang high on the hill and there was a fresh warm breeze that seemed to caress the face and delight the nostrils with heather smells and sea smells and the hints of faded-flower memories. But on an overcast, cold September afternoon, and on a Friday at that, Craig-yr-Eos was a different proposition. To start with, it lay eight miles from the Margam site. Secondly, the travelling time that should be added, couldn't be, because the building contractors for whom Jayo and Henry worked did not provide their own transport – they used the Craig-yr-Eos bus, and that ran at five-fifteen from the site. It meant that it would be touch and go whether Henry made his train back to the Rhondda. But there was one other snag: pay. While most men got paid on Thursdays at Margam, the scaffolders and a few other gangs got paid by Morris Weasel on Friday afternoon. The fact that Jayo and Henry were up at Craig-yr-Eos meant that they'd have to stop at the site office on the way back – and that made the timing even worse for Henry.

And when he saw the size of the scaffolding job ahead of them, Henry knew there was no chance that they'd be finishing early, for a three-thirty bus. There was at least three days' work at Craig-yr-Eos; at least, three by Jayo Davies standards. Even though he didn't have the excuse of having to wander off looking for clips and poles, since the job amounted to a straight demolition and new erection twenty yards away.

The afternoon sped past, for Henry was kept busy fetching and carrying, and during the break Jayo even instructed him in the art of scaffold construction. But Henry only half listened. At the back of his mind was the knowledge that he was going to be damned lucky to get the train back.

And this was one Friday night Brenda had managed to keep free.

CHAPTER II

1

Henry ordered a cup of coffee and two ham sandwiches, then waited while the hissing coffee machine summoned up the hot water to make the brown liquid that he needed to assuage the ache in his belly. It was nothing to do with hunger or thirst, that ache: Henry knew it was caused by a problem. He had felt similar aches in the past – before his finals, for instance – and now it was occasioned by the anxiety he felt over standing Brenda up. His worst fears had been confirmed, and he and Jayo had got back to the site to get paid by Morris Weasel after the other workmen had left the North Margam site. The bus was gone; the train was gone. Henry had a ninety-minute wait for the next train, and then he'd have to change before he could get back to the Rhondda.

Brenda would be furious.

He sat down near the window and sipped his coffee. He had decided against the scruffiness of a British Rail snack bar and waiting-room, and had settled for a 'bracchi' shop near the station. The name outside announced the owners were called Forgione, but in Wales all Italian-owned cafés were lumped together under the generic name of Bracchi – presumably because the early café-owners had gloried under that ancient name, Henry supposed.

Gloomily, he nibbled at his sandwich. A few girls making their way home from work caught his glance and giggled; a bus roared past, and chip-paper whirled and danced after it, discarded the night previously and now seeming to seek another owner. Henry was getting fanciful in his depression.

'Fed up, is it, Henry?'

He recognized the deep, half-Irish, half-Welsh intonation immediately. Henry looked up to see Phil Irish standing beside the table.

'I missed the train,' Henry said miserably.

'There's always another,' Phil said amiably, and walked to the counter to get himself a cup of tea. 'Been to get a haircut after work,' he announced when he returned to Henry's table. 'Goin' to have a ball tonight, so got to look presentable.'

'I was supposed to be going out as well.'

49

Phil sipped his tea noisily. 'Be too late now, I suppose. That's why you're looking so down. Girl?'

'Aye. And she'll play hell.'

'So she'll play hell! So what? Does them good once in a while, let them unsheath their claws, Henry. You don't want to worry about that.'

The thought of unsheathed claws did little to encourage Henry out of his despondency. He made no reply, and was aware of Phil Irish's eyes studying him carefully. At last the big man asked, with a certain sly intonation in his voice, 'Can I ask you something, Henry? Personal, like? How many girls you had?'

Henry stared at him blankly for a moment. 'It *is* a bit personal, Phil.'

'Aw, don't get me wrong, boy. I'm not pryin', like. It's just that ... well, you hear so much about students, the opportunities they get and all that, and I just wondered whether you took the oats that was offered you when you was at university. Or whether, since you was already fixed up at home, you didn't pick up all the cards that got dealt you.'

Henry shrugged. Phil spooned some sugar into his tea and grinned mockingly. 'This valley girl – she's got you by the short and curlies, that it, Henry?'

'I wouldn't say that.'

'Go on. I know the signs. You got tied to her before you went to university, you left the other crumpet alone even though you had the chance, and now she's only got to flutter her eyelashes at you and you get blown over by the wind. Got all the signs, you have.'

'What signs?' Henry asked, with a certain heat entering his voice, for Phil was right and he knew it.

'You got all the disadvantages and none of the advantages of marriage,' Phil said, and sipped at his tea again, this time with more satisfaction. 'You want to live a bit more, boy.'

'Like you do, I suppose?'

'Well, now you said it...' Phil paused, grinning. 'I've had a few birds, and there's more than one or two still flutterin' at my windows, knockin' their heads silly too, doing it. Now you, Henry, you got your bowels in an uproar because you can't get home to your girl in time; instead of sittin' mopin' you ought to be plucking feathers elsewhere. I could give you a hand if you like.'

'I can catch my own birds, Phil, thanks very much.'

'Don't get so bloody stiff with me, lad. Only going to suggest you come with me to The Brick Wall tonight. Good place to pull 'em, you know.'

'I've got a train to catch.'

'Aye, well, up to you...' Phil leaned back in his chair, stared gloomily out into the street, his own good humour suddenly evaporating. 'You got any idea, Henry, why that bastard Banion got a down on us?'

'Has he?'

'That overtime business. He didn't need to do that. And my pay was docked all right. And this afternoon ... but of course, you wasn't there.'

'I was up at the Craig with Jayo,' Henry explained, frowning. 'What happened at the site, then?'

'Tommy Bighead.' Phil scowled, twisting his features unpleasantly. 'The damned runt got the needle into Tonto again – he's asking for trouble, and he'll get it if he keeps pushin' that cowboy. You know them jokin' dog turds? You seen them, harmless enough, but look like the real thing. Tommy Bighead managed to sneak one into Tonto's tommybox, and bloody hell, if Tonto had got to him he'd have torn his big head off his shoulders.'

'Banion saw it?'

'Sees every bloody thing, don't he?' Phil replied sourly. 'He was down on us in three flashes and he didn't half tear a strip off us. But it should have ended there. Instead, he pulled Gareth Jenkins's crew out of Twll-Mawr and put us in. We done our screw there, and it wasn't fair to have us in again so soon. But it was like Banion's always lookin' for a chance to grind us; this one came up and he grabbed for it. Like to know why, I would.'

Craig-yr-Eos suddenly seemed salvation to Henry. He was grateful for the job that had taken him and Jayo to the clean air on the hill; he had already worked in the area known as Twll-Mawr, The Big Hole, and he was glad to have missed a second bite at that cherry. It was essentially a demolition job at Twll-Mawr, but it involved working in the sewage area for the old workings, and in semi-darkness where the imagination added significantly to the squelching filth and odorous air that had to be contended with.

'That overtime, you see...' Phil Irish seemed to have forgotten, for a moment, that Henry was even there. He appeared almost to be talking to himself. 'He wasn't on site, so how did he know we knocked off early...? And why did he challenge *me*, in particular?' Phil sat staring out of the window for almost half a minute, his brow furrowed, his slow-moving mind struggling to fathom the resentments he obviously felt that Geordie Banion held for him and the rest of the crew.

'Maybe it's just Banion's way of exerting authority,' Henry suggested.

'Eh?'

'He needs to assert himself. So he cracks down. Gives him status and power and authority. Same reason why he spends so much time up on the scaffolding. I've watched him; he enjoys the heights, because up there he's big and the people below are small. Very small.'

Phil Irish was staring at Henry with a blank look on his face, as though he had lost the drift of what Henry was trying to say. Compounded with the incomprehension was a certain wariness, as though the old suspicions that Henry saw among other workers on the site were staining Phil's eyes also – the awareness that Henry Jones was not really one of them, and never could be.

Perhaps it was the fear of losing contact with Phil, and with the group, that made Henry suddenly change his mind.

'I'll take you up, after all, Phil.'

'What?'

'The Brick Wall. I'll come with you. If I can clean up a bit.'

Phil's brow cleared. 'I can probably do even better than that.'

And he could.

Phil Irish invited Henry to take the bus with him to the digs he stayed at in Port Talbot. He lived in two rooms in a small, unpretentious terrace house whose landlady had middle-class aspirations and a working-class shortage of aspirates. She was small, stained-blonde, fluffy and pit-widowed. Phil played up to her when she flirted with him, giving her ample waist a squeeze, whispering a bawdy joke in her ear, and caressing her spreading bottom as he passed her on the stairs so that she wriggled, looked coyly adoring, and asked him with her eyes why the hell he didn't take advantage of her.

'Managed to keep her out of my bed so far,' Phil confided in Henry, 'though it's been a damn near thing a couple of times with the old whore. But she's a bloody good cook and she hasn't raised the rent this last six months – hoping she'll get payment in kind, I suppose. But that's the way, see – keep them livin' in hopes, Henry, keep them livin' in hopes...'

He had opened his wardrobe door to Henry, and after a wry glance at Henry's leanness – they were much of a height but significantly different in weight – Phil selected a pale blue shirt into which Henry could change and a pair of grey trousers which Henry was forced to support by a tightly buckled belt. A loose sweater which hid the baggy waistline made Henry, in Phil's eyes, presentable enough for an evening excursion, but he made no apology for his own elaborate dressing-up. Henry had not seen Phil off duty before, and was fascinated by the care he took with his appearance. His shirt and tie were carefully toned, and matched the flecked brown of his elegantly-cut, fashionable suit. His hair was carefully parted, and kept in place by a judicious use of hair-spray, his teeth were vigorously polished and a liberal application of both talcum powder and after-shave lotion combined with the hair-spray to surround Phil Irish with an odorous halo which on any other man might have cast doubts on his virility. In fact, there was no gainsaying Phil Irish's virility. The care he took with his appearance served only to emphasize even further the swaggering, self-confident masculinity of the man, and beside him, in the loose sweater and somewhat over-large trousers, Henry felt decidedly inferior.

But Phil told him not to worry. He could pull enough for both of them.

They took the bus down the hill to the town and Henry hurried to buy the first two pints; thereafter, Phil took over with two more pints and a couple of whisky chasers while Henry, no drinker by habit, became vaguer about where he was and who he was. Brenda became a distant figment of his imagination, unreal, not worth troubling about, and at eight o'clock, when Phil linked Henry's arm in his and marched him out into the cool night air, he no longer gave a damn about anything in the world.

The Brick Wall was already in full swing. Its external appearance was one of dilapidation, a seedy Methodist chapel that had echoed to its last hymnal paeans fifteen years ago. A short burst of activity as a bingo hall had been followed by a slide into desuetude for three years until Rhayader Entertainments had taken the lease, converted the building into a night-club, with an adjoining bar made necessary by recent legislation, and Arfon Rhayader, proprietor and general manager, had taken his first steps towards the millionaire status he intended to achieve by the time he was thirty-five, which wasn't bad going, as he explained to most people he met, for a former pit lad.

He displayed a certain wisdom, at least, in his choice of name for the club. It was officially ARFON'S, and announced itself as such in neon outside the main entrance, but a shortage of cash had meant that Arfon Rhayader had been unable to complete its interior decoration when it first opened, and behind the stage he had screened the brick wall with heavy curtaining – which had col-lapsed the second night. The stark brick wall had been exposed, Arfon's discomfiture had been en-joyed by every patron in the house, and the night-club became a success, but not as ARFON'S, in spite of what the sign said. It was, even when ornate plaster covered the back projection, The Brick Wall, to everyone who cared, and eventually Arfon himself came to advertise it as such.

Henry heard the tale as he sat at the table just above the sunken dance floor, in between two more whiskies and a nubile blonde entertainer who wore a black dress with silver spangles and insisted between songs that she was available to any man in the house who could afford her. There were no takers in spite of, or possibly because of, the vast acreage of bosom that she heaved soulfully when singing of transatlantic love. Phil shouted that he would take her on if his young friend was allowed to help, but the thought proved the last straw for Henry who, having been directed to the cloakroom, deposited with sounds of satisfaction most of what he had drunk into a washbasin. He felt like hell when he returned to the table.

'I feel like hell,' he said.

'You look like hell,' the girl said, and with an effort Henry raised his head.

She had green eyes set in an oval, rather plump face, and though her hair was even blonder than that of the nubile singer she had paid less attention to its roots, so that the centre parting she affected was dark. Her eyebrows were heavy and black in startling contrast to her hair, her eyes green-lidded, her mouth wide, smiling and generous. It was by no means a stolid face: it was sharp, alive, interested in Henry but committed to Phil Irish, and if her generous whore's mouth might show edges of discontent from time to time, it would not do so in Phil Irish's presence.

'Who are you?' Henry asked thickly.

'Helen Swain.'

'I'm Henry Jones.'

'I guessed.' She leaned sideways, pulled Phil Irish's head away from her neck and stared at him. 'He told me about you when you were in the washroom. Missed your train, he said. Wanted a good time. Seems as though he's given himself a good one while he was at it.'

'Only had a few drinks,' Henry mumbled.

'He's had two to every one of yours, and then some. All right, Phil, come up for air!'

Phil Irish came up for air, grinning, and reached for his whisky glass. Helen Swain watched him with an open affection as he finished his drink. 'You're only playing at being drunk, even now, aren't you, Phil?'

Phil Irish's eyes were bleary, but his tongue was still unslurred, even though his Irish accent had become thicker. 'You know me better than that, Helen. Gimme chance to demonstrate my prowess and I'll show you. But we mustn't forget the purpose of the visit. Came to see you, *of course,* sweetheart, but got to find a bird for little Henry here.'

'I doubt if little Henry is much interested in anything at the moment.'

'Then I'll get another drink.'

Phil rose, still light on his feet, and without another word walked in the general direction of the bar, only to swerve at the last moment to pay a call at the cloakroom first. Helen Swain watched him go, then turned back to Henry.

'Don't try to keep up with him in the drink. You'll sink.'

'I've had enough already,' Henry replied with a sickly grin. 'You ... you work here?'

She nodded. She had little crow's feet in the corner of her eyes. She was older than Henry had thought at first. 'Cashier,' she was saying. 'On the late shift tonight; finished at nine. Came in to see if Phil is going to be able to stagger back to his digs tonight.'

'It's gone nine?' Henry asked in surprise. 'My train–'

'Your train is something else again. You can forget all about that. You won't be making any train back tonight. So you might as well do as Phil intended – get drunk.'

A befuddled image of a furious Brenda drifted across his mind, like a shadowy, badly-run old film. He discarded the image with a sense of relief; if there was no train for him, he could stop feeling guilty. He looked around, willing to pay more attention to his surroundings. He turned to peer more closely at the girl beside him, but she was looking elsewhere – in the direction of the man who was approaching their table.

He wore a dinner-jacket and wore it well; his barrel chest and muscular shoulders filled the jacket until it seemed about to burst. He had a confident, proprietorial air about him as he walked among the tables, saying a word here and there, and his smile was ready and broad, white teeth flashing, tanned skin, tight-curled black hair. He did not look towards Henry and Helen Swain but his progress was designed to bring him to their table. A few moments later he was standing beside them, a big man, six feet tall, and his smile lacked warmth, held too much calculation to suit Henry.

'Hello, Helen,' the man said, and his eyes were pale blue and cold. 'Stayin' on, then?'

'That's right.' Her tone was as cold as his eyes.

'Who's your friend?'

'Just a friend. His name's Henry.'

The big man deigned to inspect Henry, and was obviously unimpressed by what he saw. 'Doesn't look your type, *bach*. Thought you liked a *man* in your bed.'

'That's why you've never crawled into it yet,' Helen said snappishly. 'But if it's any of your business, Henry's a friend of Phil and he–'

'Still knockin' around with that big Irish bastard,' the man said contemptuously. 'You ought to have more taste. You could do better, Helen.'

'It's a point of view.'

The big man in the dinner-jacket opened his mouth to speak again, but was interrupted by a wild rebel yell from near the door. He turned abruptly and his face hardened. Phil Irish had emerged from the cloakroom and was headed towards the bar, but had now slung one arm around a man's shoulder. As they lurched towards the bar Henry realized that the man to whom Phil Irish was clinging was Tonto Thomas. The big man in the dinner-jacket turned back to look at Helen after a moment. The smile was gone now and his eyes were like slate.

'We been havin' some trouble here with vandalism, as you know, Helen. Outside the club, glass smashed, signs broken, vindictive, petty stuff. But inside, so far, we've managed pretty good. But let's have it clear, girl. If that thick Irish boyfriend of yours gets so drunk that he starts taking this place apart, it'll give me more than pleasure to take *him* apart. For all sorts of reasons.' He flickered a quick glance in Henry's direction as though to check that his message reached Phil Irish's friend as well, then he looked back at Helen. 'Tell him, won't you!'

She made no reply. After a moment the dinner-jacketed man moved stiffly away, the smile returning, dispensing insincerity among the crowded tables of the night-club. Henry watched him go.

'Who the hell is he?' he asked Helen at last.

'Arfon Rhayader,' she replied shortly. For a moment the name did not register with Henry; she placed the emphasis on the second, not the first syllable of the surname, in a way Margam people sometimes did. Then, as she went on, he understood. 'Owns the club, and likes to think he owns everyone who works in it too. But he hasn't managed to mark me in the book yet and it niggles him, like.'

She subsided gloomily into silence as they both waited for Phil Irish's return. He came back some five minutes later with two pints of beer and a gin and tonic in his hands, and a reluctant Tonto Thomas in tow. Tonto, like Phil, had dressed for the occasion: his thick hair was smeared back blackly from his forehead, his dark, long-jacketed suit and drainpipe trousers were enhanced by a black string tie, and under the jacket Henry caught a flash of a wide silver-buckled leather belt. Tonto looked like a toned-down version of a Mississippi gambler, except for the pint of beer he held in his hand.

''Lo, Henry,' he said. 'Slummin', is it?'

'He's havin' a drink with his friends,' Phil said and waved his hand towards a chair at the next table. 'Now, you get that and join us, spend some of your ill-gotten gains, you bloody crook.'

What little friendliness had appeared on Tonto's mean face was fading fast, and he shook his head. 'My brother and his mates are joinin' me, so I'll grab this table over here, like. Home from the Army, he is, so you understand, don't you, if I won't join you? But thanks for the beer, of course.'

Phil batted a hand in Tonto's general direction and turned his back, dismissing Tonto from his presence. Helen leaned forward as Phil sat down. 'Now go easy,' she said. 'Rhayader's been over, and he'll be watching you, waiting for a chance to throw you out.'

'Throw *me* out?' Phil's voice rose an octave at the very thought. 'That bloody poof?' He grinned suddenly and engagingly, chucked Helen under the chin, then leered in Henry's direction. 'That Rhayader, he's been sniffin' at Helen's skirts, you understan', and he's got all uptight 'cos she's not liftin' them for him. He'd like to have a go at me, but he's scared, great poof—'

'Phil, don't underestimate him—'

'—but any time he wants to, I'll take him on. One hand behind my back... For Chrissake, Henry, drink up, lad, you're fallin' behind...'

Time seemed to drift. The noise from the group on the stage seemed to consist of a rhythmic beating that reverberated in Henry's skull. He had the vague impression that Phil and Helen left him for short periods, maybe to gyrate among the men and women on the cramped dance floor, and he distinctly recalled being fondled by some woman who looked vaguely like the earlier cabaret act, but as the beer took its effect upon him again everything became cloudy and unreal and Brenda was in his mind waving a banner aloft and the noise in his head grew to a crescendo as lights flashed, drums thundered, the walls vibrated from a cacophonous roaring boom and he heard someone shout violently before glass smashed high, a

62

light, deadly sound, and someone screamed, above the uproar. And the shout came again.

'I said, *you Irish bastard!*'

3

Once, in an old book Henry had picked up in the Cardiff library, he had seen an old print of a series of *Poses Plastiques,* the Victorian idea of culture for the masses, semi-nude men and women depicting on stage Victory, and Death, and the Dream of Empire. It came flashing back to his mind now, irrelevantly, as he stood, swaying on his feet beside the overturned table, staring at the tableau presented before his startled eyes.

They and the whole room seemed to be in a state of suspended animation. Helen Swain stood perhaps two feet from Henry, white-faced, her mouth like a gash of scarlet, her fists clenched, raised in front of her bosom. To her left was Phil Irish, with his back to Henry.

There were two men facing Phil Irish. One was Tonto Thomas, white-faced and mad as hell, but standing back for all that. The other man was not standing back: he was of much the same build as Tonto, but whereas Tonto stood out in his Mississippi gambler garb, this man was notable for the fact that he was in uniform. In spite of the befuddling effect of the liquor, Henry caught sight of the shoulder flash, and gained the impression it was the Welsh Guards. But his attention swung back almost immediately to the tableau itself and the menace it held for the group and the whole room.

In that moment Phil Irish launched himself. There was nothing catlike in his spring; he went forward like a maddened bull, surging wildly, swinging crazily, hurling himself at the man in uniform. The soldier was not as drunk as Phil and used his wits, trying to sidestep the Irishman and bringing up the beer glass into Phil's body. He was too slow, nevertheless; Phil's onslaught carried him hurtling straight into the soldier and backward, driving both of them and Tonto in addition on to the table. It exploded beneath them, legs buckling under the crashing weight of the three men, and several women started screaming as glasses shattered under the crashing bodies, beer flew in the air, and another table went over. Henry began to lurch forward unthinkingly, but Helen grabbed at his arm, pulled him away. He caught a glimpse of three burly men pushing forward with the determination and physiques of the Pontypool front row, and as Helen tugged again at his arm he allowed himself to be propelled across the room towards the wall. He caught one last sight of the three men plunging into the middle of the fray, all arms and legs, and then the noise was fading and the lights were dimmer and he smelled cigar smoke, was aware of thickly curtained windows.

'Restaurant,' Helen said hurriedly. 'Closed tonight. Come this way, through the lounge bar, and we can get outside away from the trouble.'

'What about Phil?' Henry asked dazedly.

'Oh, *Phil!*' she snapped, as though that explained everything.

The lounge bar was also closed, for redecoration, but Helen, knowing the way, led Henry through the bar, out through the far doors, along a carpeted passage and past a vast mural, half finished, before they found themselves in the entrance hall of the club. A small, worried-looking man with thin shoulders and a grey face was standing there and she approached him.

'No, just a couple of people came out,' Henry heard him say. 'Complainin' about the fightin', but that's all. Quietin' down in there now, it is. Be all right in a minute, *bach*. Go back in then, if you like, through 'ere, or back through the bar. No, that big Irishman hasn't come out – Arfon and the boys will throw him out, though, sure enough.'

Helen came back to Henry and together, silently, they waited. Three minutes ticked past. The noise had now subsided completely inside the club; the noise of battle, at least, Henry realized, as he became aware again of the subdued thudding of the drum and the beat of the music. Helen looked at him sharply twice, as though about to say something, but bit back her words each time. She began to walk up and down in the entrance, her steps short and nervous, a mother hen anxious about her chick. Then she swung around. Her lips were garish again in her white face.

'*Henry,*' she said, almost gasping the word, and then she turned, walked almost blindly back into the carpeted passage. Uncomprehending, Henry followed her, but she turned left at the end of the passage, away from the clubroom. She opened a door, crossed through a small office, and slipped the lock on another small door in the far wall. Henry felt a draught of cold air. He followed her;

she was standing stiffly in the doorway.

They were at the back of the night-club. Henry was aware of the odour of rotting food waste, the smell of dirty dustbins, and he put one hand on Helen's shoulder to lean forward and peer out around her. There was no moon, but Henry could make out, dimly, that they were facing a narrow alley that ran between the club and the block of small shops that were adjacent to The Brick Wall. For a moment he was puzzled, and then he realized that this would be where the kitchens put out their bins for collection, and although he could make out little at first, as his eyes grew accustomed to the darkness he thought he could make out the shapes of dustbins lying on their sides, scattered along the length of the alley.

But some of the dark shapes were too tall, and they moved.

Henry felt Helen's shoulder quiver and the movement was echoed by a twisting feeling in his gut. There were at least three men in the alley, big, dark, heavy-shouldered. They were standing still, looking down at something on the ground, and there was something about their lack of movement that was infinitely menacing. At their feet Henry could make out a shapeless bundle, and as he thought back to the scene in the night-club he could guess what it was. Helen's shoulders began to shake and he tightened his grip on her. He was about to slip past her, step out into the alley, when one of the standing men turned and looked directly at them.

There was a moment of silence as he stared at them, then he turned his head again, muttered something low to the other two and they walked away from the bundle on the ground, past Henry and Helen, to the kitchen door some twenty feet down in the alley. They glanced incuriously at Henry as they passed but said nothing. There was a brief flash of light as they opened the kitchen door; when it closed behind them, the last man moved, walked up to Helen and Henry.

It was Arfon Rhayader.

'Your boy-friend's back there,' he said harshly. 'You can take him home now.'

'*Diolch yn fawr*,' Helen Swain said in a bitter irony. She made to thrust past Rhayader but he flashed out a hand, gripped her by the wrist. She struggled briefly to free herself, but his grip was strong.

'Don't get stroppy with me, missis,' he said. He paused a moment, because his breath was rasping in his chest, part emotion, part violent activity. 'He asked for what he got.'

'Took three of you to do it, though, didn't it?' she taunted him.

Arfon Rhayader was silent for a moment. Henry thought, fancifully, that his eyes seemed to glitter in the darkness of the alley as he glared at Helen Swain. When he spoke, his voice was thick. 'It wouldn't take three – I could do the job myself, and thoroughly, but then I'd do it for good, see? But if I laid into that thick Irishman myself I'd half kill him, and I didn't want that. Professional job, I wanted, so I put the boys on him. Good at that they are. So you tell him this, when he comes around. We kept off his face this time, but if he ever shows it in my club again I'll see his nose spread between his ears!'

'If he doesn't spread yours first!'

Her hand came up as he squeezed her wrist in a spasm of anger, but she did not cry out. 'I'll tell you this, you bitch,' he said, 'you can collect your cards end of the week, too. I don't know what it is, but I been stupid about you and I'm saying to hell with it. It's a funny thing, but ever since you joined the staff at the club I been dogged with trouble. It's like you put a jinx on the place. Vandals bashing up the front of the club; someone smashing the bogs to bits. And the kind of bloke you shack up with, in preference to men who could do something for you, is the kind I don't want in my club. So take your *twp* Irishman, and get the hell out of my club too. Maybe my luck will change then, and things get straight again.' She snatched her hand away, and he swore. 'Stuck-up bitch; I can do without you.'

There was something in his voice that belied his last statement, nevertheless, and as he walked away on stiff legs Henry wondered, through an uncomprehending haze, whether Arfon Rhayader was angrier with himself than with either Helen or Phil Irish – angry with himself for wanting her so badly.

But Helen was already running down the alley towards the bundle on the ground.

4

'I still don't know what happened exactly,' Henry complained.

His head was aching and he felt vaguely sick after struggling up the stairs with the drunken, semi-conscious form of Phil Irish. Helen had called a taxi to the club and she and Henry had struggled out with Phil, piled him into the cab and they had driven back to her flat. The taxi-driver had seemed disinclined to offer assistance – he had, he explained, been vomited over by too many drunks in the past, so it had been left to Henry to do most of the carrying and dragging up the stairs to the first floor where Helen had her three rooms – a living-room, bedroom and kitchen.

When Henry repeated his complaint, she stopped washing Phil's face and looked up sharply.

'Make some coffee, for God's sake!'

Shamefacedly, aware he was doing little to help, Henry rose, walked into the kitchen and filled the kettle before plugging it into a wall socket. He quickly found the jar of cheap instant coffee and he heaped some of the mixture into three mugs. He added milk, and watched the coffee congeal thickly; when the kettle boiled, he poured the hot water on top of the mixture and stirred vigorously. His stomach moved, but he felt sure the coffee would do him good. He found a tin tray and carried the three mugs into the living-room.

Helen was sitting on the arm of the settee staring down dispassionately at Phil Irish. As Henry came she looked up and shook her head. 'I don't think he'll be wanting coffee. He's out like a light. My God! Men!'

She accepted a mug from Henry, then gestured him towards the easy chair in the corner of the room beside the electric fire. She rose and switched the fire on, then took a sip at her coffee, sat down in the easy chair opposite Henry and glared at Phil Irish's recumbent form, stretched out along the length of the deep settee, one foot on the floor, the other draped inelegantly over the arm of the settee.

'Just bloody typical,' she said sourly. 'He gets drunk, starts a fight, ends up in an alley getting his ribs kicked in, I worry myself sick, we struggle like hell to get him back here and all he damn well does is snore away sound as any baby.'

Henry stared at Phil Irish's torso; Helen had opened his shirt and the red, angry marks were visible along his chest and ribs, but there were no cuts or lacerations, and apart from some bruising under one eye, Phil's face also seemed relatively unmarked. 'Do you think anything is broken?' Henry asked doubtfully.

'Shouldn't think so. Arfon's boys are experts. They put the boot in where it hurts, but so that complaints afterwards are difficult to prove. They'll have taken their satisfaction, and Arfon will have put a few fists in himself; to work off some of his temper, but they'll have done no serious damage. This time.'

'You mean–'

'It's a warning,' she said, tiredness creeping into her tone. 'Phil'd better not go back to The Brick Wall. He'll try to, just to show he isn't scared, but he'd better not. Arfon's too mad to let it go.'

'But what *happened* in there?' Henry insisted.

Helen Swain looked at him, and a certain softness came into her eyes. It was as though she recognized Henry's relative innocence in this world, and perhaps she was remembering a time when she hadn't known her way around too well either. She smiled, and it was a warm, kindly smile. 'Henry Jones,' she said quietly, and it sounded as though she liked the name.

'You haven't answered my question,' Henry said after a little while, nettled in a way he could not explain to himself, or understand. 'All I remember–'

'Is very little, I bet.'

'I remember Tonto coming in, and Phil buying him a drink.'

Helen looked at Henry over the rim of her coffee-cup. 'You know that cowboy, then. His brother, too?'

Henry shook his head. 'Don't remember even seeing him – unless he was that soldier.'

'He was that soldier, all right,' Helen said, shaking her head regretfully. 'And that was the cause of all the trouble. Apparently, Tonto Thomas's brother is in the Welsh Guards and rather proud of it. Moreover, he's recently served a spell in Northern Ireland, and he's got some pretty definite views about the Irish. A couple of remarks and this silly clown here–' she glanced, half affectionately, half angrily, in Phil's direction– 'he started playing the fool. Kept singing low, like, 'The Wearing of the Green' and all that damned nonsense. I mean, he hasn't been to Ireland in fifteen years! But things got a bit heated in the end, though I tried to shut him up, and an argument started, Phil knocked over Tonto's drink when he tried to get between them, and the next thing Tonto's brother was calling Phil names. Nothing bad, but all Phil wanted was an excuse. Typical bloody Irishman. Loves a fight. But he picked the wrong place to fight in tonight.'

'And the alley?'

Helen grimaced. 'Arfon Rhayader is proud of his club. When the fight started he sent in his chucker-outs. He should have set them on Tonto and his brother as well, but he settled for Phil, who was roaring, fighting drunk by then. A fight goes to his head bad as drink, it does. Besides, Arfon had other reasons to want to hang one on Phil.'

She paused, her head down, thinking. Henry watched her, caught a glimpse of an older woman yet again, an experienced, worldly-wise, sad woman who had seen streets and gutters beyond Henry's comprehension. 'One of the reasons will be you,' he said quietly.

She looked up, smiled briefly. 'Not as drunk as you made out, were you? Aye, Arfon has been wanting to crawl in the sack with me ever since I started at The Brick Wall – God knows why.'

'You're an attractive woman.'

Her glance was quizzical. 'There are *young* girls in the club he can – and does – lay. But all right, maybe he wants me because I won't have him. Some men are funny that way. Get obsessed, they do.' A shadow passed over her face suddenly as though her words had opened up old wounds, touched exposed nerves, but it was gone in a moment. 'Anyway, he knows about me and Phil, and I suppose since he thinks that with more money than Phil that makes him a better man, he can't understand why I'll go with Phil and not with him. Don't suppose he ever will understand. More'n I do,' she added, with a laugh as she glanced at the Irishman's snoring, inert form.

'You known Phil long?' Henry asked.

'Couple of months. Met him in a pub one night. I was lonely. It started. But you – what are you going to do now? Tonight, I mean?'

Henry was startled. He glanced uncertainly at his half-empty coffee-cup, then around the strange room with its faded curtains, worn carpet, old settee and chairs, and stained wallpaper. 'I ... well ... I'll just finish this and then I'll go see if there's a train home I can get.'

'Only train you'll get now is to Cardiff. Through Bridgend. If you get off at Bridgend it's a hell of a walk, and though you might get a connection up the valley from Cardiff, it's unlikely. Only one thing for it. Stay here.'

'But–'

'Don't worry, young man. We'll keep it proper. You can have my bed.'

Henry's eyes widened. 'But that's soft! You have the bed, and I'll sleep out here on the floor.'

Helen Swain was grinning at him. 'Proper cavalier, aren't you? There's nothing soft about it. *You* have the bed, because there's just no way we can get this big lunk here to move off the settee. And if I know him – and I do – with that much drink in him he's bound to wake up in the middle of the night and feel for a woman. It's as well that I'd be on the settee with him, not you.' She paused, and grinned again. 'You're blushing, Henry.'

He knew he was *not*. His face was flushed with the drink, or maybe it was the coffee, but he was too damned old to blush. It was true she affected him in a strange way, as Brenda for instance did not affect him, but that had nothing to do with blushing.

'Anyway,' she was saying, 'you can take the bed and I'll stay out here with this great clown. Thing is, I'll have to strip some of the blankets off the bed to cover us, but if you feel cold in the night there's some old ones in the cupboard in the corner of the bedroom. I don't use them – they're flannel sheets, really, but doubled they're warm as blankets. You can use them, all right, if you need them.'

She finished her coffee, took the cups into the kitchen and washed them. Henry walked out behind her, after a little while, and watched her. She had put on a small apron, and it made her seem younger, somehow, and more vulnerable.

'You been livin' in Port Talbot long?'

She glanced back over her shoulder and smiled at him, shook her head. 'About three years, I suppose. I had a cousin up the road from here; stayed with her for about a year, then she went off to Canada, and I got some digs, then, finally, this flat.'

'Where'd you live before here, then?'

'Nosey, aren't you?' She placed the cups in a drying rack, wiped her hands on the apron, took it off, folded it and placed it on the hook beside the gas cooker. She brushed past Henry as she walked into the living-room and he caught the faint odour of her fading perfume. She stood in the living-room, staring at Phil Irish, and a note of regret crept into her voice.

'Oh, I lived around about a bit, I can tell you, before I came here. I'm twenty-eight, Henry, but I look older and that's because I've seen enough life and more for some women twice my age.' She glanced back over her shoulder. 'You know where I was raised?'

'No.'

'Cardiff. Bute Street. Heard of it?'

'I know Bute Street.'

'Used to have an evil reputation. Changed after the war, of course. Cleaned up, they said. But to me it was always a stinking place. And I got out first chance. Even then, I was sixteen before I made it. And for what!'

She walked forward, tugged at the cushion that had slipped under Phil's shoulder, pushed it back under his head. 'Always did pick the wrong ones,' she said. 'Like Phil, here. Why the hell don't I shack up with Arfon Rhayader for a while? At least he'd shove a few quid my way, while it lasted. But what'll I get from Phil? A good time, a lot of laughs, and some great loving... It wasn't what I expected when I left Bute Street. Wasn't what I got either.'

She swung around, bustled Henry towards the bedroom.

'Come on, let's get you sorted out.'

She stripped the coverlet from the narrow bed, pulled away two blankets and piled them in a heap on the floor, and then replaced the coverlet. Henry followed her back into the living-room, carrying one of the blankets, and watched as she folded them around Phil.

'You got married when you left Cardiff then?'

'That's right,' she said in a business-like voice. 'Got married at eighteen–'

'But you said–'

She grinned at him. 'You'll never make a ladies' man if you keep catching them out, Henry. All right, I left Cardiff and *lived* with this feller for two years, and *then* we got married. A year later I left him, got the hell out of Liverpool, and took a job in a factory in Stoke. Couple of years there, and back I came to Wales.'

Henry was puzzled. 'You lived with him for two years, then left him after he married you? That doesn't make sense.'

'It made sense to me,' she said grimly. She hesitated, glared at Henry, and then added, 'Look, it's none of your damn business anyway, but the fact is we *got* married because I thought it would help things, get things sorted out. It didn't.'

'How do you mean, sort–'

'He was a jealous, possessive man who made life hell for me; I married him eventually because I thought it would help. It didn't. He was still jealous, still possessive – and he still kept asking me too many questions. Like you do. Now go to bed!'

Henry went to bed.

As he lay in bed in the darkness he heard her moving about lightly in the living-room. The light shining under the door went out after a little while, and he thought of the warmth of Helen Swain, her body curving against the bruised, sleeping, drunken body of Phil Irish. He began to shiver slightly at the thought; an hour later he was still shivering and he realized he was cold.

He threw back the coverlet and stood up. He tried to grope his way towards the cupboard in the corner but had lost his bearings so he reached for the light cord above the bed and pulled it. The light was dazzling. Not wishing to disturb Helen next door he moved quickly towards the cupboard.

The old flannelette sheets were piled on a shelf at the top of the cupboard. He was clumsy as he pulled them down; they came all together, with dust, and a cardboard box that opened as it fell and spread a conglomeration of rubbish on the floor. Henry cursed. He picked up two of the sheets, folded them hastily, and stretched them over the bed to provide extra warmth. Then he turned back to the mess on the floor.

There was not a great deal of it really, and in fact Henry thought it rather pathetic. There were some tiny china shoes, imitation Dutch clogs, that a little girl might have worn as an ornament for a dress. There was the cover from a box of matches, labelled with a restaurant name in Cardiff. There were a couple of newspaper cuttings, one announcing a death, and he did not read the others. All the rest consisted of similar paraphernalia, ranging from used bus tickets to a lock of hair, the faded ephemera of a dead past. The letters were few and tied with a piece of cord. He put them back in the box, with the rest of the items. The last thing he replaced was the photograph; last, because it had fluttered behind the cupboard door. He picked it up, inspected it, and saw it was a wedding photograph. It was a snapshot, not a professional print, and the subjects were squinting into a bright sun. They were too far from the camera for Henry to see the faces clearly, but he was pretty sure the girl was Helen Swain. The tall man holding her arm possessively must be the man she married, Henry thought. Swain. He wondered what his first name was. Tall, slim, handsome, standing awkwardly, a little grim for a wedding day. Maybe he was hanging on to her like that so she didn't run away.

Henry put the snapshot back in the box and replaced the box in the cupboard. He climbed back into bed. Tomorrow he'd get the early train back to the Rhondda.

He was still thinking of the smiling girl and the tall, awkward man in the photograph when he went to sleep. But he dreamed of Brenda, and she was furious.

5

If Friday had been bad, Monday was worse.

Tommy Bighead was at the station for the early train and he was in a bad temper. He was niggly, and anxious and angry in turn; his tongue was sharper-edged than ever, and he seemed spoiling for a fight. Henry openly avoided him when the train came in, for he had his own troubles. Nan had been upset that he hadn't told them he wasn't coming back on Friday night, and she'd been stiff with him all weekend – even though there was no way, short of sending a telegram, that he could have informed her. Because she was stiff with him, she was worse with Granda, and Granda was angry at *that,* so he went for Henry again on Saturday night about the job in the bank.

Then, having seen nothing of Brenda on Saturday, Henry had gone around to her home on Sunday morning. She had been quite precise.

'I simply see no point in continuing our present relationship. I am not going to make myself available as and when you feel inclined to spend some time with me. There is no reason why you couldn't take a good job in the valley, a job that would offer you prospects, a good salary, a secure professional future. I just don't understand you. Your grandad has told me what he would like you to do – after all, we had to talk about *something* when you didn't turn up on Friday night and I wasted a whole evening, hanging about for you – and I simply cannot understand why you don't take his advice, accept his attempts to help you. But if you want to stay on at Margam, if you want to waste your life, if you want to spend half of your working days in travel, well, don't expect me to be waiting around for you all the time.'

Everyone else seemed to be in a similar argumentative mood on Monday morning. Henry was surrounded by petty, squabbling comments. It was a heavy, overcast morning, and there was a hint of thunder in the air, so perhaps it had something to do with the weather, but Henry felt that something was going to burst before the day was out.

He had expected to be going out to Craig-yr-Eos with Jayo again, but Geordie Banion met them as soon as they clocked in with Morris Weasel – who gave Henry a vicious, angry look as though he wished him a million miles from Margam – and told them that there was a more urgent job to be done in Twll-Mawr. Jayo just shuffled his feet, but Henry groaned openly and Geordie Banion turned on him like a terrier after a rat.

'What's the matter with you, sonny? If the work's gettin' too much for you, why don't you get back to your books? Playin' around here is one thing, pretendin' you're one of the world's workers, but if the going's tough you can always pull out, can't you, not like the rest of us! All right, but if you want pay at the end of the week you bloody work for it – and if I say it's Twll-Mawr, that's where you damned well go!'

Taken aback by the sheer virulence and vindictiveness in Banion's tone, Henry attempted to stammer a reply, denying he was merely treating North Margam employment as a game, but Banion was disinclined to listen. With a contemptuous shake of his head he turned away, a fine line of spittle on his lips. He strode awkwardly across the site to the hut used by the site foremen as Jayo tapped Henry's sleeve silently and began to shamble, head down, towards Twll-Mawr. It was to be dimness, bad air and worse smells for the rest of the morning.

The time went on, one bad-tempered hour after another. Jayo and Henry were alone in Twll-Mawr; some foundations had been dug at the far end of the great hole, but it was necessary to raise some ceilings and remove several concrete joists, and scaffolding was required for the demolition men to get the work done. For once, Henry and Jayo worked without stopping, and this time Henry was happy about Jayo's silences, for he felt too angry to talk. Some two hours after they had started they heard some vague shouting from above their heads, and then Tonto Thomas's head appeared, framed in the entrance to Twll-Mawr. It was difficult to make out his features from the bottom of Twll-Mawr, for the light was behind him, but the crude anger that scored his voice was obvious enough.

'Phil Irish down there?'

Henry shook his head. 'No.'

'I'll break the bastard's neck when I see him – if I don't break Tommy Bighead's first!'

He moved away, swearing obscenely. Henry turned around to find Jayo standing just behind him, still looking up towards the entrance as though wishing he were up there in the brightness of the day. Henry walked past him, picked up a six-foot length of scaffolding tube and carried it across to the pile he had been collecting.

'That's not the way to do it,' Jayo Davies said quietly.

Henry stopped in surprise. It was not often that Jayo Davies actually started a conversation. 'Not the way to do what?' he asked after a moment.

'Tonto Thomas would just put the boot in,' Jayo said, turning away from the light falling through the entrance. 'That's not the way to get his own back on Tommy Bighead. I'd do it different, like.'

'You?' Henry said stupidly. Strangely enough he had always thought Jayo Davies incapable of such commitment as to 'get his own back' on anyone. He was too shy, too introverted, too self-effacing to act in such a manner. And yet, Henry realized, he did not really know Jayo Davies at all

81

well. The man kept to himself, and so did little to expose his inner self to his workmates.

'Got reason, got plenty of reason,' Jayo said quietly. 'That Tommy Bighead, he's made a lot of enemies on the North Margam site, you know. Not just Tonto Thomas. Ever tell you about my neck, did I? Before you came to the site, it was. Fibreglass. It was left over from some insulating material they was using, see, and Tommy Bighead sprinkled some of it inside my shirt. Bloody silly thing to do, wasn't it? Scratched my neck to ribbons. Had to take time off work ... missed a couple of shifts, I did. Just because that silly little bugger wanted to play jokes. Nothin' jokin' in that, though, is there? Under the doctor, I was. Bad. Said he never did it, of course, but I know Tommy Bighead, see, and he did it all right. Get my own back one day, I will. But quiet, like; not the way Tonto Thomas would. Best way, see. Not shout the odds like Tonto, but just do it, put the boot in, or whatever, when nobody's looking, like.'

Jayo paused, suddenly aware that the venom of his tone was being communicated to Henry. He stared at Henry for a moment, then dropped his glance. There was something panicky in his voice when he said he was going off to look for some clips, as though he feared he had exposed his soul to Henry, and he shambled off. Henry, uninvited, made no attempt to follow him. Instead, he sat down on a broken beam, angry, despondent, and wondering not for the first time what the hell he was doing here among these people, doing this job. A confused welter of emotions had brought him here – pride, disgust, contempt for the society

82

he was doomed to join – but now he had made a point yet couldn't break away. For in a sense, if that's what it was all about, merely making a gesture, the whole thing had been worthless right from the start. It had to be more than a gesture; it had to mean something.

Jayo did not come back during the next twenty minutes. Henry checked his watch. It would soon be time for break. It was true that Jayo occasionally wandered off like this, but generally speaking he returned before break so that he could appear to emerge having done some work immediately before the whistle went. Well, the hell with it, Henry thought. Time for break had almost arisen anyway.

He got up and headed for the ladder. There were four entrances to Twll-Mawr – two of them served by iron ladders stanchioned to the walls, the other two entrances being nothing more than air-and-light holes that sent down pools of light to relieve the dimness. In the sixty-yards length of Twll-Mawr such entrances were inadequate and accounted for the warm stuffiness of the air. Henry walked to the first ladder and climbed up. As always, the sky seemed bright on coming out of Twll-Mawr, but the clouds were still piled up and the weather was still heavy and thundery.

At the top of the ladder Henry looked around, but there was no sign of Jayo. As he stood there, the whistle blew, so he walked immediately over to the concrete ramp where he and the rest of the group took their rest. He had sat down and poured himself a mug of coffee before he realized that there was still no sign of the others.

Henry leaned forward, looking around for the rest of the gang. There was no sign of them. But Morris Weasel was coming towards him. He stopped some thirty yards away and shouted to Henry.

'Tonto there?... Jayo?... Phil Irish?'

To each name, Henry shook his head. Puzzled, he watched Morris Weasel turn away bad-temperedly to stamp along among the broken buildings, looking for the gang. But the break was half over before any of them appeared, and then it was Tonto, his narrow mean face scowling, and obviously in no mood to talk. Henry left him alone. Shortly afterwards Henry caught sight of Phil Irish, half hidden by the sheds to the right. He was arguing with someone, and when Phil finally made a chopping motion with his hand, as though ending a conversation, and turned away, the other man became visible to Henry. It was Tommy Big-head. The little man called something after Phil, and the Irishman hesitated, then nodded angrily and marched on towards the ramp.

He sat down heavily, grunting, and after he reached into his knapsack for his sandwiches he rubbed a hand along his ribs. Henry raised his eyebrows.

'You all right now, Phil?'

'Awright.'

'I'm sorry I didn't stop to have a chat, see how you were. My train was early Saturday morning, and you were still asleep, so rather than wake either of you I–'

His voice faded as he became aware that Phil was looking past him, his brows ridged heavily.

84

Henry had almost forgotten that Tonto was there with them, and had played a part in the Friday night battle. The silence was suddenly electric. At last Phil Irish growled, 'Anythin' you want to say, Tonto?'

'Not about this, I haven't. But it's time you started thinkin' before you swung a fist, you big dumb Irishman—'

'I don't take much provokin', Tonto,' Phil Irish said in a rumbling warning. 'Not this morning.'

'If you want to finish the fight you started on Friday, that's all right with me, you ox! But let's get one thing clear. We can settle our quarrels off the site – I'm not risking my bloody job as well as the—'

'Shurrup, Tonto. You always had a big mouth.'

'My big mouth, is it? What about your stupid skull? The reason why we're in this mess now—'

'*I said Shurrup!*'

There was no mistaking the controlled violence in Phil Irish's tone now, and it beat through to Tonto. They glared at each other for a long moment, then Tonto cursed and threw away the dregs from his coffee mug with a violent gesture. He thrust it into his knapsack and rose without another word, stalking away from Henry and Phil. The Irishman watched him go, and there was fire still in his eyes.

'What the hell's got into everyone this morning, Phil?' Henry asked irritably.

'Monday,' Phil Irish grunted, and deigned to say nothing more.

Jayo was not down in Twll-Mawr. Henry hung

around for a little while unhappily, waiting for the scaffolder to appear, but after a further twenty minutes there was still no sign of him and time weighed heavily on Henry. He was at a loss what to do. He could stay down in Twll-Mawr all morning but no work would get done. He could wander out looking for Jayo, but that way Jayo might appear while Henry was wandering about, and how could he explain that if he came face to face with Geordie Banion? Alternatively, he could check with Banion; there was the chance that Banion had already ordered Jayo elsewhere. That must be what had happened; Banion had seen Jayo – he saw everything on the damned site – and had given him another job, and Jayo had omitted to tell Henry. A surge of unreasoning anger rose in Henry; he could get blamed if that had happened; Banion had already crossed swords with him once today, and if he caught Henry without work, the fat would really start to splutter. That was it, Henry determined: he'd find Banion, *tell* him he was down in Twll-Mawr twiddling his thumbs, and let Jayo Davies and his skiving go to hell. Why should Henry cover for him, after all? He'd done too much already, keeping his mouth shut while Jayo skulked around avoiding work.

Henry climbed out of Twll-Mawr. Thunder rolled above his head, and far away, out beyond the coastline, there was a distant flash as lightning crackled in the sky. Henry waited for a few moments, and soon there came another rumble. There would be a storm; he knew it.

He looked around. The site seemed almost deserted. The air was full of the usual site noise –

rumbling of machinery, distant voices, lorries, excavations, the thumping steam-hammer, the crushing of rock under bulldozers, dust and dimness and the hum of activity – but somehow it was all muted, screened by an atmosphere that was thick with something Henry could almost *feel*. The thunder clouds piled up in the sky until they seemed to be lying above the site like a great animal waiting to pounce. Henry looked across to the tall scaffolding, and the rising blocks of steel and concrete, and he walked about and he saw no one, no one he knew.

Somewhere up above there the roofers were at work. Perhaps Banion had asked Jayo to go up to the roof. Henry reached for the scaffolding and began to climb. It was always hard – and awkward – work for him, but today it seemed worse. His hands slipped on the smooth iron, his boots scrabbled noisily for a foothold against the iron clips. Painfully, he made his way upwards to the third floor, and he craned his head backward to look up for signs of activity. There was none.

He was on the scaffolding on the north side of the tower block; he edged his way along until he could turn the corner to the east side. From there, at this height, he could look out above the activity of the site itself, over the grey dunes to the sea. Some days Henry had watched it up here and the sea had been so intensely blue that it had made his eyes ache. Today, under the cloud pall and whipped by a slow heavy breeze, it was black, grey-tipped, and menacing. Henry looked away and began to climb along the east side of the block.

Until he felt the breeze pass him. Yet it was not

a breeze.

Something lifted and moved in Henry's chest as the thought passed through his mind, and almost at the same instant he heard the appalling crash below. He looked down and was seized with a sudden, violent vertigo. The ground seemed to shimmer before his eyes, the buildings began to sway, and he clung on as though for his life. But through the nausea he still saw the dust rising from below, a slow, deadly dust.

And where there had been a small shed, immediately below him, there was now only a pile of timber and rubble.

It had been a small shed, Henry thought, as almost without realizing what he was doing he began to make his descent. A small lean-to, corrugated iron roof, timber and concrete supports, a wooden door that was locked to prevent kids stealing the tools that were left there overnight by labourers. Strong enough to deter children from breaking in, it had never been built strongly enough to withstand a blow from ninety feet from above.

The light was bad, fading fast. Henry felt a spot of rain on his face and he paused, looked up to the sky. It was leaden, heavy, and the thunder rolled again as he saw, beyond the dunes, the first driving squall of rain. In a matter of minutes it would be lashing the North Margam site. Henry tried to go faster, but he had always been slow on the scaffolding.

There were voices down below him, and the rain arrived, driving in over the site in long slanting curtains. Henry reached the ground, dropping the last six feet, and he turned, the rain dashing into his face. He saw a small group of perhaps five, or maybe six men. They were pulling away the timber piled on the ground, all that remained of the shed. The corrugated roof had already been dragged away, and as Henry watched, coming forward slowly, he saw Geordie Banion pushing others aside to lift a wide sheet of plywood that must have stood inside the shed door, against the wall. And he saw Banion stagger, lurch in surprise. Then he looked back, and around him, and his face was greyer than the thundery skies above. The rain streamed down his face, and his greasy cap dripped water while his normally emotionless face was twisted with something Henry could not read.

Then Henry looked past Banion to what lay on the ground, and he understood. He had felt the breath of that thing as it had whistled past him on its downward path, and now it lay there, massive, cracked, but deadly, a concrete joist from the roof ninety feet above ground. Deadly, for under it lay something that Henry recognized after one long, horror-stricken moment. Not by its face, but by its short legs and powerful upper body, for the encephalitic head of the malicious little man from the Rhondda had been completely and comprehensively smashed.

CHAPTER III

1

Next day a bright sun had cleared the sky, there were birds singing high, and from the tower Henry could see a freighter headed Swansea way, black and squat against the sharp blue of the sea. The dunes looked inviting, a long, rolling golden stretch of sand clumped with small green patches where tough grass had attained a precarious foothold for a while, until the winter storms would eat away at their roots and cause them to start their painful clinging process all over again.

Nearer at hand there was much activity. The usual bustle of the site continued, sharpened now as an air of subdued excitement spread amongst the workmen, and there was a tendency during break for men from other parts of the site to wander towards the destroyed shed where Tommy Bighead had died. Two television vans, the local press and a radio team had come out last night, and had been packing up when Henry arrived at work; now, the momentary interest that the little man's death had caused was dying, with just one reporter remaining on site to check on the police statements. For the official word was out: Tommy Bighead's death was probably accidental.

Even so, the police were still on the roof, and the shed itself at the foot of the block was still

90

screened off from prying eyes. The roofers had been kept away, and during the first hour Henry, attached to another scaffolder since Jayo had not turned up for work, had been able to see people in plain clothes – forensic experts, he supposed, creeping about on the roof doing unimaginable tests on the equipment and materials there. But even they were now preparing to leave, and soon the roof would be deserted.

'Looks as though we'll be able to get on with some bloody work soon,' the voice said behind Henry's back.

Henry turned around, startled, and was some-what discomfited to realize that Geordie Banion must have seen him standing there idly, watching the activity of the forensic scientists across the way. He bent self-consciously to pick up a scaffolding pole, but Banion seemed hardly aware of the movement. He was staring at the roof, and the men preparing to leave it, and his eyes were like agate, his thin, handsome face set sternly, his lips compressed in a tight line. Unreasonably, Henry once again felt himself, in the presence of an omniscient being, and so he was startled by Banion's question.

'What do you think happened over there yester-day?'

'On the roof?'

'Where else?'

Henry swallowed and stared across to the men now leaving it, as though hoping for some sign that would give him an appropriate answer. 'The whisper on the site is that a bolt gave way, a stanchion broke, the concrete joist fell by accident and hit the shed. A one in a million chance.'

'One in a million chance that Tommy Bighead was inside that shed,' Banion said softly, frowning. 'He had no official reason to be in there.'

Henry was silent and Banion remained standing there for a long moment. Then, abruptly changing the subject, he said, 'Jayo Davies isn't in this morning. What time did he leave the site yesterday?'

'I don't know. We were down in Twll-Mawr, and he just … went.' Henry hesitated, not wishing to cause trouble for Jayo Davies. 'I couldn't be sure of the exact time. You … you think he went home then?'

'Not paid to think. Not paid to answer questions, either,' Banion added gloomily, 'but I've had to, like the others. Your turn now.'

'How do you mean?'

'They want you. The police. Questions.'

Henry stared at Banion open-mouthed. 'But I've got nothing to tell them!'

Banion turned to glare at him directly. The greasy cap was pulled well forward on his forehead and gave him an even more hawkish look than usual. His eyes seemed to bore into Henry as he said, 'How do you know what you've got to tell them till they ask? They asked me questions, and I told them things I hadn't even realized I knew! They've already seen that cowboy mate of yours, and the Irishman, and me: there's just you and Jayo Davies now. So down you go.'

'But–'

The eyes bored hard into him. 'You were on site when Tommy Bighead died. You were on the scaffolding, I understand, when the joist fell. They'll want to ask you about it. So tell them, son. Tell them all you know. It's the best way. Tell them, even if it causes problems for other people. I've had to do it. Even though I didn't like it. So get on down there. Who knows, maybe you can answer the questions I couldn't. That's how they get their facts, isn't it? Fitting answers together – like jigsaw puzzles.'

Banion turned away abruptly, waving dismissal to Henry, and walked in his awkward, splay-footed fashion across to the scaffolder to whom Henry had been assigned. As he explained where Henry was going, Henry began to climb down the scaffolding. He felt a great reluctance to face the police, and his heart was thudding uncomfortably in his chest; it meant that his progress down the scaffolding, normally slow, was slower than ever this morning.

As he reached the bottom, a man standing near by came forward. He was young, dressed in a dark raincoat.

'Henry Jones? Come on, the Super's waiting for you and he doesn't enjoy being kept waiting.'

Detective-Superintendent Morgan didn't *seem* to mind that Henry had kept him waiting. He was a big man, heavy in the jowl and florid of countenance, with little piggy eyes that were never still. He oozed the kind of affability that Henry knew to be insincere, the type of friendly good humour that could be turned on and off as circumstances required, and Henry guessed that in appropriate conditions, and with certain kinds of people,

Morgan would prove to be an overbearing, over-powering bully.

But right now he was affable. He invited Henry to sit on the ramshackle chair in the cabin behind Morris Weasel's office, where he and his detective-sergeant had set up an inquiries room, and suggested, after a little small talk, that Henry should tell all he knew.

'Where should I start?' Henry asked helplessly.

Detective-Superintendent Morgan smiled indulgently. 'Tell me about yourself first,' he suggested, and leaned back behind the deal desk.

Henry told Morgan about himself. He explained that he was a graduate, and when pressed, explained the discipline in which he had graduated. Inevitably, Morgan's heavy eyebrows rose, and a knowing look was sent in the sergeant's direction. Defensively, Henry went on to explain that he was uncertain about a future career so he had decided to work at North Margam. Temporarily, he added, under Morgan's prodding, and inside him a little something wriggled and died. Maybe it was an illusion.

Morgan asked him about the crew he worked with, and suggested he give a thumbnail sketch of each of the gang – after all, as a sociologist, he would be more aware than some of what made men tick, and how they behaved in social situations.

Henry tried. He remained, as far as possible, on ground strictly neutral. He touched upon Tonto Thomas's meanness but not to excess; he advised that Jayo Davies's behaviour was largely due to an intense shyness; he made the guess that Phil Irish, though slow-witted, was no fool, and though it might take him a while to reach a conclusion, he'd get there in the end.

'And Tommy Bighead?'

Henry told him about Tommy Bighead. At first he hesitated, his Nan's insistence that one should not speak ill of the dead echoing at the back of his mind, but under the shifting, quick glances of the detective-superintendent facing him across the cheap desk, he allowed himself to expand. He spoke of the little man's malice, about his practical jokes, about the fact that he was so intensely disliked on the site.

'Disliked enough to be murdered?' Morgan asked quietly, and Henry's head came up with a jerk.

'I thought it was an accident!'

'So it may be, so it may be,' Morgan soothed him. 'We just don't know yet. I've had a look at the roof and it could well be it was just an accident. But until I've had the usual reports from forensic I can't tell, can I? The factory inspectorate will be up there this afternoon to carry out an inspection to see whether any civil liabilities arise, and it's likely they'll be clobbering the firm, or the roofing contractors, or both. But whether or not Tommy Bighead's relatives can claim compensation is none of my business: I'm just interested in the criminal situation. If there is one. And the way you tell it – and for that matter, the way others have talked about the little man as well – it seems to me he wasn't exactly the best-liked man at North Margam.'

It needed little encouragement for Henry to try

to defend Tommy Bighead; he felt it unfair that the man, now dead, should have all his worst qualities described without some attempt at balance being achieved. So he tried to tell Morgan how he had seen Tommy Bighead – the frustrations that had lain inside the man, the pressures, the need to strike out at a normal world that despised him and laughed at him. Morgan looked thoughtful as Henry explained, and the detective-sergeant scribbled away busily in an open notebook.

'Interesting,' Detective-Superintendent Morgan said when Henry finished, then added slyly, 'Sounds as if you was the only one who really liked him.'

'That's not true,' Henry said. 'I liked him no more than anyone else. But I felt sorry for him ... and I think I understood him better than most people. That's all.'

Morgan cocked his head on one side, considered with an air of wisdom, then nodded. 'Okay. So much for background. Let's get down to the meat now then, shall we? Tell you what I want, Henry. I want you to go through the morning – as you saw it – minute by minute. Who you were with, who you saw, what they said, what they did, and take me right up to the time you found the body–'

'There were others there before me,' Henry protested.

'Up to the time you arrived where the corpse was lying, then,' Morgan conceded, 'and then tell me what happened after.'

'Nothing happened afterwards that was relevant!'

'Then tell me what wasn't relevant, and let me decide on the status of the information,' Morgan said, and his tone was a little sharper as though he was getting tired of the affable detective-superintendent act. 'After all,' he added, softening again, 'you know about people, but I know about *facts*, isn't it?'

When Henry climbed back up the scaffolding to return to the roof on which he had been working, he found his new mate idle, leaning on the low parapet at the edge of the roof, staring across at the deserted roof from which the concrete joist that had killed Tommy Bighead had fallen. He turned around as Henry approached. He was a dark, stocky man with the kind of chin that always seemed unshaven and usually was.

'Finished then?'

'Yes.'

'Gave you a good grilling, did they?'

'I suppose so.'

The man shook his head, turned back to stare across to the other roof. 'Coppers all left there now. Got all they need, I suppose. Won't be much, I bet. Don't reckon they'll let the roofers back for a while, though.'

'Superintendent Morgan told me the factory inspectors will be looking at it this afternoon,' Henry said.

'Aye,' the scaffolder said vehemently. 'And *they'll* find trouble too.'

'How do you mean?'

Henry's mate was only too eager to explain. 'Well, I'll tell you. I was in the pits, see, for ten

97

years before I decided to get out. During the time I was there I learned up all about the regulations. There was a chance, see, that I might get a union post in Merthyr, strong union man I am, so I flogged up all I could on regulations so I knew what I was talking about, at meetings as well as at the face. Got to impress the boys, you have, if they are going to vote for you. Anyway, to cut a long story short, I know a fair bit about the factory regulations – bit different from the pits, but not a lot...' He paused wistfully. 'If those bloody pits hadn't closed down, I could have got that union job too; closed down too soon they did, blast the Coal Board.'

He stared at Henry blankly for a moment, as though he had lost the drift of his conversation in the fogs of past resentments, and then he waved an arm around him. 'Look at this roof,' he said.

Henry looked. 'What's wrong with it?'

'That's the point. Nothin'. Look at it; it's a one-storey addition to the existing building, right? Flat concrete roof and ceiling; concrete joists; breeze blocks; walls over there where we're fixing the scaffolding for the next extension. Now what's that over there?'

Henry stared obediently in the direction in which the man pointed. 'Guard rail?' he asked hopefully.

'Right, boy. In accordance with the regulations. Gimme time and I could probably give you chapter and verse, but maybe it's regulation twenty-four or twenty-eight, can't remember exactly. Fact is, it says if a bloke has to work any place where he's likely to fall more'n six and a half feet, you got

98

to have guard rails and toe boards there to stop him goin' over. We got 'em here. But,' he added triumphantly, 'look across there.'

Henry looked to the other roof. 'No guard rail.'

'An' no toe boards. Least, not against the edge where that joist went over.'

'*Went* over?'

The man scratched his face and his fingers made a harsh rasping sound against his chin. He grunted, screwed up his face thoughtfully, and shook his head. 'Aw, come on! Plain as the nose on your face, it is. That was no accident that killed Tommy Bighead.'

'But the police–'

'They'll play it careful, like, until they got more information, and it's that chap Morgan in charge, isn't it? Used to watch him play for Cwmavon, you know, and I don't suppose he's changed. Front row, he was, and he used to get up to every dirty trick under the sun when the ref wasn't lookin' his way. He'll be the same now; won't say anythin' till it suits *his* book to say it. And maybe it suits him to say *accident,* now like.'

'But how can you be so sure?'

'Stands to reason, boy, if you just look at it. This roof here is finished, right? But you can still see how it's fixed. Concrete joists, bolted together – see those iron bolts? And then these breeze blocks here. Now look to that roof over there. See, the roof advances half-way along – just to where they got those ladders lashed against the apex. Right? And against the toe board over on the far side of the completed roof they got breeze blocks and joists, piled and stacked ready for use. Right? Now, that joist that killed Tommy Bighead, it fell from the open side, the area without the toe board, okay? How many spare breeze blocks and joists can you see on that part of the roof?'

Henry shrugged, counted. 'About half dozen units, I'd say.'

'And how far are they from that open edge?'

'Six, ten feet maybe.'

'And where are they going to be fitted into the roof?'

Henry frowned. He stared carefully at the roof. The chasm that remained to be filled in the roof over which he and Geordie Banion had walked a few days ago lay in the centre, away from the edges.

'You see what I mean,' the scaffolder said scornfully, 'you see it, don't you? None of the roofers would have been using the joists at the *edge* of the roof. There'd have been no reason for them to work *outwards*. You can't see a broken joist anywhere, can you? And they wouldn't have been stupid enough to place the joist *right* on the edge. Look at the others, for Chrissake. Ten feet in. No. Can't convince me, you can't. Overbalance, nothin'. Someone up there, he lifted one of them joists, stood it on end, toppled it right over. And I bet you a quid the cops will be sayin' that within twenty-four hours. Tell you, boy; believe me.'

He turned away, began to march back towards the scaffolding, ready to carry on with the work he had left. Over his shoulder, he said, 'Another question, of course, as to *why* it happened. Unpopular little bastard, by all accounts, but you got to be *bloody* unpopular, haven't you, to get your head crushed in by a lump of concrete. Couple of hard men I wouldn't mind doin' it to, mind you. Like that Tyneside foreman of yours, for a start...'

Henry was hardly listening. He was thinking about Detective-Superintendent Morgan. A devious, dirty front row player for Cwmavon. Henry wondered how far he had carried his methods into his police career and guessed it might well be a long way. And if Morgan really did think it was a case of murder, some of the questioning he had subjected Henry to now began to seem more probing and more relevant than Henry had suspected. The information about the other members of the gang, for instance. But more importantly, the last few questions Morgan had asked him.

'Tell me, Henry,' the detective-superintendent had said, 'when you were up on that scaffolding, did you *see* anything? Like Tommy Bighead goin' in the shed, for instance?'

'No. I was too busy looking up; I was climbing, you see.'

'Hmmm... And you didn't see the joist fall?'

'No. Just felt the wind of its passing.'

'That's right. You said before. And you didn't see any of the roofing gang, or anyone else, up above you?'

'No. I saw no one.'

The florid face had peered carefully into Henry's before the last questions were asked. 'And Tommy Bighead – did you have a chat with him that morning? Did he mention the money he had on him, in that chat?'

Henry had been puzzled. 'No. I hardly spoke to him yesterday morning. We didn't travel together.

But ... I don't understand ... what money are you talking about?'

'Well, I'll tell you,' Morgan had said confidentially, leaning forward and dropping his voice. 'It's not something I want spread around, you understand, because I got some more inquiries to make yet. But there's something I don't understand, see. Tommy Bighead, well, you heard that Max Boyce song about the bloke who gets crushed to death on the Carlisle motorway, and his pal's upset because his international ticket was in the dead man's pocket? Funny song, that. Well, maybe Tommy Bighead had a buttie on the site who'll be similarly placed. Not over a ticket. Over the matter of a hundred and fifty quid. That's right. That's what Tommy Bighead had in his pocket when he died. Tight roll of flyers. Funny, isn't it? In view of his usual wage packet, some might even say inexplicable, like.'

2

The death of Tommy Bighead had had various repercussions on the site, not least in the general tightening up of supervision by the foremen. Geordie Banion was more active than ever, moving among the buildings, clambering over the scaffolding, emerging out of some of the hideholes that men like Jayo Davies habitually used, checking on scaffolding security, testing clips, shaking poles, dragging down personally structures he regarded as dangerous. The bosses had obviously been on the site manager's back, he had chased up O'Connor so that even *he* appeared on site, and the foremen were hopping around like fleas on a scratching dog's back.

It made life uncomfortable for the men, though the older hands said it would soon pass. A site accident always had that effect. But the roofing gangs did not return up aloft, and later in the afternoon the factory inspectors came and did their preliminary inspection. Within the hour it was all around the site. They would be 'clobbering' the management, the builders and the roofing contractors for breach of the building regulations. The defence of the roofing contractors was that the guard rails and toe boards had been removed only the day before the accident because they had been makeshift anyway, but that made no difference. The site was in trouble – and that meant everyone.

A couple of detective-sergeants and an inspector still poked around that afternoon, but Superintendent Morgan drove off, either to follow a line of inquiry or get a good lunch – opinion on the site was divided. But Henry felt decidedly unhappy. He could not be sure how far he had really been taken into Morgan's confidence, and it worried him that he might have been set up by some sort of confidence trick by the detective. The matter of the money, in particular, bothered him. It was odd that Tommy Bighead had been carrying so much – and on a Monday. But to what extent was the information common knowledge? Had Detective-Superintendent Morgan really told Henry alone, or did others know about it? Henry pondered on the matter and decided there was one person at least who might know something about it.

He saw him at the end of the afternoon break.

He was wandering around the site as usual; on this occasion he came shinning down some scaffolding like a dark little monkey, his jacket flying open so that he seemed to have two black wings, and when he reached the ground and looked around in his usual shifty-eyed way, Henry walked across to him.

'Hello, Mr Morris. You still looking for Phil?'

Morris Weasel failed to meet Henry's glance. 'No, just checking, just checking. Part of my job, see.' He patted his torn waistcoat, where he kept his little black book. Henry could think of nothing more to say, momentarily unable to consider a way in which he could bring the conversation around to the desired topic, but Morris Weasel seemed equally uneasy, and equally unwilling simply to walk away.

'You ... ah ... you seen the police, then?' Morris asked at last, with an air of unconcern.

'Yes. Have they interviewed you, Mr Morris?'

Morris Weasel scratched at the ground with his left boot. 'Aye, we had a bit of a chat, like. What they ask you?'

'General stuff, mostly. Wanted me to tell them exactly how the day passed, that sort of thing.'

'What did you tell them?' Morris asked sharply.

Henry stared at him in surprise. 'What was there to tell them? I mean, I just told them I was working here and all that.' It was an odd experience; Henry had wanted to try to get from Morris Weasel admissions that did not necessitate giving anything away himself; but it was

Morris who was making all the running.

'Did they ... did they ask you anything about–' Morris Weasel hesitated, as though struggling for a word – 'about...' He started again, finding the word, and then discarded it, as though deeming discretion wiser than suggestion.

'Money?' Henry offered.

He was immediately surprised by the reaction from Morris Weasel. The dark, narrow head shot up, the shifty eyes searched his features, the mouth twitched nervously as though suddenly affected by a tic.

'What do you mean, *money?*'

Henry opened his mouth to make a non-committal reply but Morris went on, 'Did they ask *you* about money matters then? What sort of money matters? What did Griff Morgan want to know, damn his eyes!'

Henry shook his head slowly. He had no answer to his own questions, but he was reluctant to take the conversation further; Morris Weasel was in a nervous state, but he was keen to pump Henry, and Henry was not prepared to break Detective-Superintendent Morgan's 'confidence'.

'I just thought,' Henry said, 'that you'd be interested to know whether Morgan asked about money – I mean, it's your job, isn't it, paying off the men and so on, and I just thought...'

His voice faded and died as Morris glared at him. He had the feeling that Morris was scared about something, and part of the fear was concerned with what Henry Jones could do to Morris Weasel – and it was a thought that completely baffled Henry.

The query remained with Henry after Morris slipped away and disappeared in the general direction of his office. Henry went back to the scaffolding, but his mind was only half on the job. Towards the end of the afternoon his mate, having completed the task assigned to him by Geordie Banion, advised Henry that he was going to 'get lost' on site, and he suggested Henry did the same.

'And for God's sake, I hope you've learned somethin' from Jayo Davies. You ought to have done. Master at it, he is. So just keep out of Banion's way until the whistle goes – and if he does find you, you're just lookin' for clips, all right, boy?'

With a sly wink the scaffolder left Henry to his own devices. It was quite a responsibility, having to hide away so that Banion did not see him, particularly since if Banion found Henry he was sure to ask awkward questions about Henry's mate. So Henry decided uneasily to do as the man had suggested and learn from his experiences with Jayo Davies – find a hole deep enough and quiet enough to hide for the hour or more remaining of the shift.

Henry picked up a scaffolding pole at the foot of the tower block, hoisted it to his shoulder, winced as it touched the sore muscle, and then plodded slowly along, aimlessly, but hoping that it looked as though he were working. He thought for a moment of heading for Twll-Mawr, but it was likely that there'd be a crew down there. So what he really wanted was a suitable bunker, where some scaffolding had been done recently; if Banion then appeared Henry could pretend he had been collecting materials. But his mind was a blank; he could not remember the location of a bunker that fitted.

He spent ten minutes in a quiet corner behind some timber stacks, but it was not restful; if Nan could have seen him she would have said he was like a cat on hot bricks. He was unable to relax; he kept looking skywards to check if there was any possibility of Banion, up aloft somewhere, seeing him; he kept walking to the edge of the stack and peering around it surreptitiously, to see if anyone was approaching. In the end the whole game got so much on Henry's nerves that he decided to move away and find a better hideaway.

He remembered one of Jayo's bunkers at last; some three hundred yards from Morris Weasel's site office, it was screened from most of the site by a new hopper, and though the bunker was only ten feet square and unused he could take some scaffolding clips down with him, and pretend, if caught, that he had climbed down to fish them out. When he reached the bunker, a swift glance around convinced Henry the coast was clear; once he was down there, in the semi-darkness, his conviction faded and he almost began to bite his nails at the thought of Banion.

And yet, what the hell! All Banion could do was give him a dirty job like Twll-Mawr – or sack him. And maybe a sacking would be a good thing, anyway. Wasn't it time for Henry Jones to swallow pride, salvage a life style, forget principle?

With still thirty minutes to go, Henry could stand it no longer. He had been sitting on some boxes stacked in the corner of the bunker but his nerves were raw; he had to get out of the bunker, and to hell with the scaffolder he was supposed to be working for. If Henry was caught skiving, that was bad luck. He shinned up and out of the bunker – and with a huge sense of relief saw Phil Irish some thirty yards away.

Phil had his back to Henry and was walking away from him at a rapid pace, but to Henry the Irishman looked like salvation. He could attach himself to Phil; help him do whatever he was doing; ease away the last half-hour without the strain of pretending to work and doing nothing. Henry almost ran after Phil Irish, as the man disappeared around the corner, past the chimney.

It was an old chimney that had served as a smoke outlet for the brickworks that had had a brief life on the North Margam site. It had been one of three, but the others had collapsed, and now it stood alone in a line of kilns that looked like so many little huts with iron doors, shoulder to shoulder, brick-built, solid, not yet attacked by the bulldozers still clearing this part of the site. But there was no sign of Phil Irish.

Henry was puzzled. He stared around in the warm sunshine of the afternoon, and for a moment he fancied a chill wind touched his back – the fanciful breeze of fear at the unexplained. Then his logic took over and he grinned: Phil would have walked past the hutments to his right and was somewhere down there. It was only a matter of climbing on top of the kilns, to get eight feet above ground, and Henry would have a vantage point from which he'd be able to see Phil.

It was easily done. Henry walked to one of the

destroyed chimneys and climbed over the bricks that had collapsed there in a pile, until he was level with the tops of the kilns. Then he simply walked across on to the kilns and stood behind the broken chimney, feeling the air move slightly, cool, out of the old chimney as he scanned the hutments for Phil Irish.

Until the chill wind touched his back again and he was afraid.

When he was a child it had been the creaking of boards in the middle of the night, the dark at the top of the stairs, a shadow on the ceiling when all the house was asleep. Later, when he had taken to reading horror stories, it was an occasional Henry James or Algernon Blackwood shudder that had taken him momentarily or a longer Edgar Allan Poe nightmare that had disturbed his sleep. But this was different, because he was a man, and the sun was still in the sky and he was surrounded by the realities of life – machinery and people and buildings.

When he heard the sibilant, menacing whisper again, however, his skin still crawled and he looked wildly around him. Even as he did so he realized that the sound was not behind him, or all around him; it was merely a freak, a sonic trick that was being worked on him unconsciously. The whisper came from the broken chimney to his left, and it was the faded remnants of a conversation that was going on somewhere within the construction beneath his feet.

Henry stared down along the line of kilns. He was puzzled. He could not imagine why anyone should want to enter the kiln themselves – if that was even possible. There was a boiler room at each end of the line of kilns, approached in each case by steps leading below ground level, and Henry guessed that workmen might enter those if they wanted to do a Jayo Davies and avoid work. But Henry certainly hadn't heard of anyone using the kilns as hideaways, and the boiler rooms would probably be locked anyway, since they were in a dangerous state and scheduled for demolition.

He stepped nearer the stack. The whispers were thin, attenuated, and in a curious way out of phase. It was as though one man was interrupting another and then repeating himself quietly – the conversation had a surrealist touch about it, and it was several moments before Henry realized what caused the lack of phasing. It was echoes – the voices were being picked up in the kilns, echoing through air vents, and escaping, with further echoes added, through the chimney, faded, dissociated, almost unintelligible.

Almost, but not quite.

'Jones... Henry... Henry Jones...'

The hidden conversationalists were talking about him.

Henry stood stock still, rigid with shock. It was, in his imagination, like being present to watch his own death. The name was his but it was so divorced from reality as to raise prickles on the back of his neck. A distorted image from a broken mirror, a ghostly whisper from a deep well. 'Henry Jones...'

Henry leaned over the stackhole and craned his head down to the stone to listen. It was impossible to guess who was speaking, for the voices

110

were stripped of their tones and inflections. All that came up through the chimney was a collection of odd words, meaningless, and yet the more frightening for all that. With difficulty, Henry tried to piece the words together, against the still echoing, fading background of his own name. Each word came through at least three times, fading, but after a moment Henry's ear picked up the rhythm of the echoes and was able to select from among the confusion.

'*...knows ... materials ... fifty quid ... ardour...*'

The words were fairly clear but they made no sense. Henry clung to the brickwork, but the words were fading, and he realized that the conversation had ended. He looked about him, to the clouds rolling up from Swansea way, and to the warm brown bricks of the kilns, and his mouth was dry. His hand was shaking slightly, and he could not understand why. He felt that he was getting involved in something that must remain none of his business, and yet his name had been mentioned, and money ... and Tommy Bighead had been carrying a wad of notes when he died.

'*Jones!*' This time it was not a whisper, but a mighty bellow. Startled, Henry lost his grip on the brick chimney and almost fell, but he caught his balance at the last moment, and looked back behind him. Fifty yards away, between Henry and the hopper, was Geordie Banion, arms hanging down at his sides, glaring at Henry as though he thought he was mad.

'What the hell you doin' up there? Don't tell me there's poles down that hole, now!'

Hurriedly, Henry clambered down over the

brick pile and picked up the few clips he had left at the foot of the kilns. Banion was striding towards him purposefully, his long legs jerking as he came, his fists clenched. O'Connor and the site manager would have been on the backs of the foremen today, and Henry would have some explanations to make as far as Geordie Banion was concerned. Henry waited until the foreman approached, his hawk face set grimly under the greasy peaked cap.

'Where's your mate?' Banion asked.

Henry's mouth was dry and he swallowed hard. 'He ... he sent me to get some poles, collect them up in a pile, ready for the next job. Said he'd be doing the same. He–'

'Bloody skivin', more like it. Like that damned Jayo Davies. Think I don't know about these things, don't you? Hell, I've worked all over, man, Manchester, Liverpool, Cardiff, Hartlepool, Sunderland, Llanelli – you think I don't know the game yet? Tell you what I *don't* know, though, son. I don't know what the hell you was doin' on that chimney.'

The cold eyes glared into Henry's, and Henry was silent. He shrugged inanely, unable to raise an answer, and looked around him for salvation. Banion snorted, then brushed past Henry, sending him staggering, climbed up on the piles of bricks, made his way to the top of the kilns and stood there like a great evil spider, long legs splayed, hands on hips, as he swivelled slowly, looking about him. He put one hand on the broken chimney and turned to look back to Henry. He stared at him for a long moment, seemed about to say

112

something, then stopped. He looked down, and along at the line of kilns. He frowned, looked at Henry again, and his eyes glittered suddenly.

'All right, Jones. Push off.'

Henry did not understand, and his face must have shown his incomprehension. 'I'm letting it go this time,' Banion said. 'Now shove off.'

No slanging match; no orders as to what he should do; no further questions. Puzzled, Henry walked away with the clips, and when he looked back Banion was climbing down from the stack. Henry reached the hopper and glanced back again; Banion was standing twenty feet away from the kilns, beside a broken wall some four feet high.

It was, Henry considered, a useful wall if a man wanted suddenly to conceal himself.

3

Henry thought about the whole thing during the train journey back to the Rhondda. It was inexplicable, the whole series of events. The death of Tommy Bighead seemed to have created a situation where events no longer occurred in logical fashion. It was as though the concrete that had smashed down on the little man had disjointed the times so that men were no longer related to their surroundings. Phil Irish disappearing; whispers in a chimney; Geordie Banion's strange behaviour; Morris Weasel's fear and anxiety; Detective-Superintendent Morgan's 'confidence' – there must be some sort of logical pattern behind it all, even though Henry felt generally that life never really fitted into logical patterns at all.

His own conduct, for instance. Where was the logic in it? He had a degree, yet he worked on a building site – and one which was two hours away from home at that. Where was the sense in that? Yet it had seemed right at the time, and now there was a certain pride that refused to allow him to accept he had been wrong. A man had to make a stand at some time, show that he was not to be tied down like an animal for branding.

But when he saw Brenda standing outside the station waiting for him he was suddenly near capitulation.

It had been a fine day and she was taking advantage of the warm evening air to wear one of her summer dresses with a light blue jacket over her arm. She had loosened her reddish hair so that it lay long down her back and she looked younger and more serene than he had seen her for a long time. He was made aware, as he had not been aware for months, of the days when he had first met her, five years ago, and there was the smell of crushed fern in his nostrils, the warmth of a summer sun on his back and a moving body under him.

'Surprise,' he said, and she smiled, hesitated, then took his hand.

'Nice or otherwise?' she asked carefully.

His own body moved. 'Nice,' he said, and she squeezed his hand lightly.

They walked hand in hand down the hill from the station and a couple of workmen grinned at them as they strode past. Perhaps they were remembering a time when their own sweethearts had waited for them; certainly, there was a knowing look in their eyes that suggested times would change for Henry once that girl got him to the altar. Henry cared little for their knowing glances; he was *glad* Brenda had come to meet him. He was confused, and she was something stable in his life, someone he knew, and understood.

'I thought I was a bit ... abrupt on Sunday,' Brenda said.

'You had every right to be annoyed.'

'No, let me get it off my chest,' Brenda insisted. 'There was no way really you could have got in touch, and I know you didn't stay back intentionally. I was just mad, I suppose, because my evening had been wasted and I didn't see you. But then to say I'm not going to see you any more, well, that's soft, isn't it? I mean, it's cutting off my nose to spite my face, like, isn't it?'

Henry laughed, and put his arm around her. She resisted for a moment, thinking of her clean dress against his workclothes, but as evidence of her mood she then moved closer, happily, to him.

'Anyway, how's things gone today?'

Henry screwed up his face. 'Everything's tightened up, since the ... accident yesterday.'

'What, security procedures, you mean?'

'That's right. But it's been a funny day all round. Police saw me.'

Brenda's body stiffened and her head turned so that she could look at Henry closely. *'Police?'*

She had all her working-class background suspicion and fear of the police and any involvement with them. Hurriedly, Henry tried to explain. 'It was just routine, that's all. You know, they were

115

making inquiries about all the people who knew Tommy Bighead, and what they'd been doing when he got killed, all that sort of thing.'

She didn't understand, and said so, and in his further attempts at explanation something of Henry's own confusion at the day's events must have crept through because Brenda's blue eyes got wider and her plump face became more stained with suspicion the longer Henry went on.

'It *was* just an accident, wasn't it?'

Fatally, Henry hesitated, then compounded the mistake. 'The man I was working with today has his doubts.'

'*Henry!*'

The police alone was bad enough. The thought of violent death horrified Brenda. And stimulated her. Colour came to her face, a subdued, irrepressible excitement entered her eyes. 'What's *happened* today, Henry?'

And as they walked hand in hand past the Workmen's Institute and the new multiple store, over the old railway bridge and up past the Boys' Club, skirted the decayed tennis court and walked through the grounds of the Anglican Church of St Peter, Henry told her. It was stupid, and he should have known better, but he told her – not only the details of his interview with Detective-Superintendent Morgan, but all the rest. He was in full flight before he noticed how her reaction was changing.

'But you see,' Henry was saying, 'it's the whole unrelated sequence that's bothering me. It's like having hints dropped all around you, and being unable to pick them up, make sense out of them, create a logical whole. I always thought I was a logical person, but I can't be. For I'm sure there's something in all this that provides the kind of connection – a key to the whole business. I–'

'You got to leave,' Brenda said snappishly. 'Today.'

'What–'

'You're not going back to Margam in the morning.'

Henry stopped, turned, faced her. He didn't like what he saw; when she had that kind of determined look in her eye it boded ill for Henry Jones. 'Now what are you on about, Brenda?'

'It's bad enough being involved with the police,' she said. 'What on earth people will say in the chapel when they hear, I don't know. That's bad enough in itself, but what's worse is a continuing involvement – and that's what you'll have if you stay there.'

'But I can't just up and leave!'

'Why not?'

'Because ... well, because it would look suspicious!'

Brenda released his hand; her breath was coming quick now, but not the way it did when they made love. 'I don't know what you're trying to say, Henry.'

'Well...' Henry cast around vainly for a moment. 'Well, look at Jayo Davies, for instance. The police are bound to be wanting to see him. Bound to be suspicious as to why he hasn't been in to work today, and left early yesterday. They'll be out looking for him. Now if *I* leave as well, next thing is they'd be coming here to the valley to have a talk with me, and I'm damned sure you and your family and the chapel wouldn't like *that*, would they?'

'You've already told the police all you know,' Brenda said suspiciously.

'But *they* don't know that.'

'There's something funny going on here.' She began to walk on, her steps jerky, a little unco-ordinated, angry. 'I been trying to get you to leave Margam, and now that you really ought to, you still insist on going back.'

'You don't understand, Brenda. This thing will blow over; there'll be an explanation. It was probably Phil down in the kilns, for instance, and my name came up casually–'

'What have you got involved in, Henry Jones?' Brenda's tone had become harsher, scored with a dangerous inflection that was compounded of suspicion, fear and dislike. 'I don't want anything to do with a man who gets involved in anything criminal.'

'*Criminal!*' Henry stared at her for a moment, and then almost laughed. 'Now come on, Brenda, don't get all high horse with me, *bach*. Depends what you mean by criminal, of course, but let's take your old man. Singing his heart out in chapels on Sunday, then taking bets for that bookie, down in the Con Club, rest of the week.'

'That was ten years ago,' Brenda flashed at him. 'It was before the gambling laws got changed.'

'But it was against the law,' Henry insisted. 'It was *criminal*.'

'But that's *different*. Even Sergeant Griffiths used to have a bet with him! But we're not talking about that, anyway, you're just trying to confuse me, change the subject again. Ten years ago that was and it wasn't *really* criminal. Not like killing people.'

'I haven't said–'

'And not like *stealing*, either!'

'Now wait a minute.' Henry put out a hand, grabbed Brenda by the arm and swung her around to face him. She stood rebelliously, her face flushed, her chin up, the light of battle still dancing in her eyes, and some of Henry's own anger began to drain away as he thought how pretty she looked. He injected more fire into his veins to counteract the effect she was having on him in her summer dress. 'Who said anything about stealing? I didn't.'

'Didn't have to, did you? Obvious, isn't it?'

'Not to me.'

'Well it is to me! Oh, I know all about those builders' labourers, and all those council workmen, and all those men in the pits. They all got to do something on the side, all got to be making a bit of money, like a habit it is, it's all corruption, I know it, I hear about it in the library, you'd be surprised what I hear. And if you stay at that bloody Margam place you'll get as bad as the rest of them, Henry Jones! It's humiliating for me, can't you see that; proud I was when you were at university, and you came home with your long college scarf and we went out together, but what have I got to be proud of now? Just a labourer you are, miles away in Margam, and can't – or won't – even *explain* to me why you do it, not in a way I can understand, anyway, and I got brains, you know! And now here you are, in trouble at the site,

and a man's been killed, and there's funny goings-
on and all you can do is carp at me, and twist
arguments, and say nasty things about my father.'

'To hell with your father!'

'And to hell with you, Henry Jones!' she
shouted, tears starting in her eyes. 'Go stay in
Margam, spend all your time in the pub like last
Friday night–'

'I wasn't in a pub,' Henry snapped back, annoyed and guilty and upset. 'I was in a night-club
and I spent the night in Phil Irish's girl-friend's
place–'

'You never told me that!' Her fury now became
uncontrollable and she clenched her fists as
though to beat at him. 'You never told me that!'

'Well, I'm telling you now and I don't give a
damn if you think the worst of me. Think what
you like. Think what you want to about Margam
and Phil Irish and his girl-friend and me, but
don't bother me with it. You've got a small, valley-
enclosed mind, Brenda, and it's dirty and mean
and narrow as the streets behind your house. If
your reasons for getting me out of Margam were
real reasons I might have got out before now – but
they're not; they're based on pride, founded in
humiliation, constructed of prejudice and snob-
bishness, and cemented by an insensate desire to
climb a social ladder that doesn't really exist and
certainly doesn't *mean* anything to real people.
But that's your trouble, Brenda – your trouble is
you're not real. You're just a reflection, an image;
you're what you think other people want to see,
and you want me to be the same. Well, I'm not
going to mould myself into any shape predeter-

120

mined by you or your mother or—'

'Oh, you and your *words!*' Brenda interrupted him. 'You're so clever, with your university education!'

'I thought it was what you liked about me. It made me a superior boy-friend, by comparison with the men the other women in the library go out with!'

'Ohhh...' Brenda struggled for almost five seconds to find the right words and then she gave in. 'Oh, *get stuffed, Henry Jones.*'

It was, Henry thought, the closest she'd got to being a human being in the last three years.

4

And she'd been right.

That was the annoying thing about Brenda. When Henry was with her he thought he desired her and loved her; away from her he was aware of her faults, the pettifogging narrowness of mind that chapel and parents encouraged, the social aspirations that would never really be satisfied in a valley that was largely one class anyway and where membership of the golf club at Penrhys was as much as any professional man could desire. He wondered whether she would go away to England with him; he could take a job, a middle-class, professional job, white collar stuff; and get Brenda a semi-detached house to keep clean in some featureless suburbia and they'd be married and have kids – and what would she say to that? Henry knew already. If he were to suggest they moved as far as Treherbert she'd complain, because she'd be all of two miles from her Mam and that would never do. Suffocating, that's what it was.

But as he looked out of the grimy train window Henry wondered also whether there was any salvation for him in Margam. He didn't really know himself, now, why he was here – if he had ever known. He needed to talk to someone about it, that was the point; it was no good bottling things up inside your chest – better to talk it out with someone who would listen and, hopefully, understand.

Yet when Henry came down to brass tacks, Brenda was right, basically. He was a son of the valley, it was in his blood and in his bones. A university education could not change that. All right, he kicked against its *mores*, but what else was there for him, when the ties that held him so close were so deeply emotional? The fact that he despised them was another matter – it was sad, but he could not cut free from them. And as far as Margam was concerned, Brenda had always been puzzled about it – and was right to be puzzled. Yet he could not explain – not to her, not properly. He needed to explain, as much for himself as any other person, but Brenda couldn't be objective. She was too tied up in the valley, and in Henry too, maybe.

As for her fear of the police, it was all so petty. She would even resist meeting a policeman socially, for fear one day a police car would stop outside her door and the neighbours would talk. And when she had stormed off last night it had certainly been with the intention of cutting free from a man who was, in her eyes, consorting with the criminal classes.

Yet was she wrong in that – or right again? Henry pondered on the matter as he joined the other workmen on the bus to travel up to the building site. There was certainly something odd going on – apart from the matter of Tommy Bighead's death. It was as though that accident – or killing – had stirred up other matters, caused ripples and reactions that were spreading wide through the site. It was inevitable, Henry guessed, but he felt as though he were part of a conspiracy he knew nothing about.

And he wanted to know about it.

There was still no sign of Jayo Davies on the site. As he clocked in, Henry asked Morris Weasel what had happened to Jayo, but Morris glared at him with an odd hostility and shrugged his thin shoulders. He didn't know, and he didn't care. Henry could see what he did care about, as Morris kept glancing over his shoulder at the police car parked behind his office.

Geordie Banion assigned Henry to work with yet another new scaffolder. He was a taciturn North Walian who immediately expressed his dislike of valley folk in the peculiar sibilant speech of the northern mountains and thereafter, as far as possible, he and Henry ignored each other. Henry wandered the site collecting materials and the North Wales man worked silently and swiftly. Henry was kept busy and his shoulders were aching by the time the whistle went for mid-morning break.

Physical activity had not dulled his brain; he

had been mulling over a number of questions, and when he saw Phil Irish at the concrete ramp with Tonto Thomas he sat beside him. They were drinking their coffee silently, avoiding each other's eyes. Henry poured his own coffee, took a sip, and said, 'I think there's something funny going on around here.'

Tonto Thomas's head swivelled; he looked hard at Henry, then his glance slid past to Phil. He said nothing, however, and Phil also was silent.

'I don't think Tommy Bighead died by accident.'

'Neither do the police,' Tonto Thomas snapped harshly. 'Talk is this morning, they think it was murder. So the screws are on. Bastards.'

He was glaring at Phil Irish in a strange way, as though he considered the whole blame lay with him for the little man's death. Henry hesitated, then turned to Phil.

'What exactly was Tommy Bighead up to?'

Tonto Thomas hissed, but it was at Phil Irish that Henry was looking. The big Irishman was calm; he took a long pull at his coffee, sighed with satisfaction, then pushed his mug into his haversack. 'Can't imagine,' he said at last.

'He was up to something,' Henry insisted stubbornly. 'And I don't know, I get the feeling...'

'What sort of feeling, son?' Tonto said spitefully, and his eyes were mean and hard.

'Leave him alone, Tonto,' Phil Irish said. Tonto Thomas stood up, grabbing for his knapsack and tommybox, and stood over them, glaring at Phil Irish. 'That's what should have been in your mind, you dumb Irish bastard, before you blew everything!'

'Shove off, Tonto,' Phil said coldly.

'If you hadn't been so bloody stupid–'

'*Shove off!*'

Tonto Thomas counted himself a tough character and at weekends he gunned down the best, but Phil Irish was a big man, and dislike and anger made poor substitutes for courage and muscle. He swore, vehemently, powerfully and obscenely, spitting out the words, but they were carefully general, carefully directed without precision towards a particular man, and they allowed him to blow off steam without risking Phil's violence. He had already tasted of that the previous Friday and wanted no second helping. He stalked off, stiff-legged, and Phil Irish put his head back against the concrete ramp, closing his eyes. Henry looked at him; he seemed to be unconcerned, but there were lines about his eyes and signs of strain at the corners of his mouth. Phil Irish was more concerned than he wanted to appear.

'So what was Tonto getting so excited about?' Henry asked.

'Too many questions.'

'And not enough answers,' Henry replied. 'Some I can guess. Like it was you mentioning my name in the kilns yesterday.'

Henry knew it was a mistake the moment he said it. Phil's, eyes snapped open and he stared at the sky for one long moment, as though his slow brain was incapable of grasping the full implications of what Henry had said. Then, very evenly, he said, 'What you mean, about the kilns?'

There was no going back on it now. Henry swallowed hard; his mouth was suddenly as dry as it had been yesterday. 'End of the day,' he said. 'I came out of the bunker and saw you walking away. I went after you – wanted to see if I could spend the last half-hour working with you, like. Then you disappeared.'

Henry paused as the Irishman's eyes came around to his. The glance was impassive, but Henry gained the impression of movement deep inside those eyes, the first slow surge of anger. 'Go on,' Phil Irish said.

'So I looked for you.' A touch of defiance entered Henry's voice. 'I climbed on top of the kilns, but I couldn't see you. Then I ... I heard this sort of whispering coming from the broken chimney. And I listened.'

'You listened...' Phil said slowly. 'To *what?*'

'I heard my name. There were two men talking. My guess is one of them was you. And my name was used. I'd like to know why!'

'Is that all you heard?'

'A few other words. Nothing that made sense. It was kind of jumbled together. But I heard my name, all right. And I want to know what it was about.'

Phil Irish frowned, and sniffed. 'Imagination,' he said.

'No. There was another word I heard. *Money.* And Tommy Bighead had plenty on him when he died.'

Phil Irish sat up. He was scowling now, and the anger was real in his eyes. 'How do you know that?' he asked.

'I know it. That's enough. What I *want* to know is why you were using my name in the kilns, who you were talking to, what money had to do with it ... and what it all has to do with Tommy Bighead's death.'

'And if I said I wasn't in the kilns, and I don't know anythin' about this money thing, and as for Tommy Bighead's death, I don't know what you're getting at–'

'I'd say you were lying.'

Phil Irish's eyes were steady now, fixed, cold. 'I got an Irish temper, you know.'

'I've seen it in action. Like last Friday. But the fact remains, I've got a right to a few answers.'

'Not from me, Henry.'

'From you.'

'Don't you try pushing me, Henry Jones. I can flatten you flatter than a pancake.'

'I still want to know–'

Phil Irish stood up. He was big against the sun, and his shoulders were broad and powerful. 'Lissen,' he said. 'Lissen to me good. There's only one thing I want to say to you, Henry, and that is – you must be mistaken. You're talking a lot of–'

'Maybe Geordie Banion was mistaken too then?' Henry said recklessly.

Phil Irish went rigid. He expelled his breath slowly, the way Henry's Granda did sometimes coming up Ton Hill, when the pain in his chest was unbearable and he needed to drag life into his lungs. After almost thirty seconds' silence, Phil Irish said thickly, 'What's Banion got to do with this?'

'He saw me on the kilns. He called me down. He went up himself and then sent me away. But last time I saw him he was all but hiding behind a wall. If you *weren't* in the kilns, fair enough – but whoever was, Geordie Banion knows who it was. He waited, I reckon, waited to see them come out. So maybe I should ask him, is that it?'

Phil's large hand shot out. His thick, powerful fingers wound in Henry's collar, dragged him up so that his face was pressed against Phil Irish's chest. Henry struggled indignantly, but was almost helpless in the fierceness and strength of Phil's grip. He smelt the sweatiness of the Irishman's shirt, was aware of the hair darkening the man's chest, and humiliation swept over him as he felt a real fear at the anger in the constraining fist.

'Don't you go asking anyone anything, boy,' Phil Irish said menacingly. 'Not me, nor Banion, nor anyone. Just remember – it's none of your business, so don't poke your nose in it. I'm telling you this for your own good. Leave things alone. Unnerstand? Do as you're bloody well told, leave things alone – and *mind your own damned business!'*

With a sore throat and a sorer temper Henry worked up aloft during the second session of the day. He was glad to get away from the ground for once; glad to feel a fresh clean breeze high in the sky, and glad to be able to work silently with the North Walian and nurse his bruised neck, his bruised feelings and his damaged ego. He felt now that he should have resisted Phil; he felt, at this safe height, that he should have shown Phil Irish that he too was no weakling. Reality was sobering nevertheless; if he had tried to resist Phil, he could have been battered to a pulp. He had already seen what Phil Irish could do and how he could behave

128

when he was in a rage. He could lose control; maybe even kill a man in a temper.

Looming larger than anything else, however, was Henry's resentment. It was a mixed emotion. A little part of it concerned Brenda; their rift still rankled with him, as well as his own inability to explain himself. But far greater than that was the way Phil Irish had handled him. It was not merely the physical violence and the threat: it was the fact that the Irishman felt he *could* frighten Henry out of asking questions, even when Henry felt he had a *right* to ask them.

For Henry there was one clear course of conduct. If no answer was forthcoming from Phil, he must seek elsewhere. For all his statement to Phil, Henry nevertheless shrank from asking Banion for his views. No doubt part of this was due to Phil's menacing, but more than that was the dislike – indeed, the fear – that Henry held for Banion. It was the traditional fear, he supposed, that any young workman had of his foreman, but it was fear, nevertheless.

And if he couldn't ask Banion, there was only one other way around his resentment. Find out for himself. Nor was that so difficult a proposition, for something was already stirring in Henry's mind. It had been sparked by Brenda's words, fanned by hints underlying Detective-Superintendent Morgan's questions, and fuelled by facts that were only now beginning to fit into some sort of logical place. Henry had been walking around the site with his eyes closed, an innocent abroad. Now things were changing, and he was beginning to see – not clearly, but if his vision was blurred, at least he could make out some vague forms.

The afternoon was busy; the scaffolder Henry was with worked methodically and swiftly and with commitment, so Henry was unable to do what he wanted to do, and try to discover some answers to his questions. After a while the initial urgency died as he considered the matter; it might be better in any case if he were to undertake the operation when the site was quiet. So he worked on quietly, and kept his thoughts to himself.

When the afternoon finally drew to a close Henry and the North Walian were still working aloft. The unfriendly scaffolder collected his things together eight minutes before the whistle went, and made leisurely progress down to the ground. Henry had intended using the excuse of taking a rest for five minutes as a reason for staying behind, but in the event it was not required; the North Walian made no enquiry as to what Henry intended doing staying behind on the concrete roof, so no explanation was necessary.

From the roof Henry could look down and see all the workmen knocking off as the whistle blew. It was faintly amusing to see how work during the last twenty minutes would seem to have drawn men near to the site office, so that when the whistle went they would have a short walk only to the main gates. They even walked out in firm time, Henry thought wryly.

After the whistle had gone the site cleared quickly. The buses pulled out, loaded with workmen, a few lorries rumbled away, small groups of men took a short break before carrying on with overtime work, but since most of that was concentrated around and near Twll-Mawr, most of the site was quiet. It would grow busier later in the week, when men who had strapped became eager for overtime to make up their wages, but right now things were fairly quiet.

At six o'clock Henry began to make his way down from the roof. He still had only vague ideas as to what he was going to do and where he was going to start, and he had worked out no methodical plan of campaign, but he had decided to work from what information he possessed, sketchy as it was. And in the first instance it involved recalling the perambulations of Jayo Davies.

He had never really thought of it before, to any great extent. Jayo was lazy, of course; he was a man who *needed* to hide away in order to break the system. But Henry had never questioned the *paths* he had taken, never queried the manner in which Jayo moved from point to point, day by day. He had assumed it was a movement dictated by the need to prevent Geordie Banion discovering Jayo's regular hideaway – it was better to be in different places rather than stick to one. There was less chance of getting caught out by the foreman. But now, Henry was about to ask that very question – he wanted to try to work out whether Jayo's perambulations formed a pattern on the site.

The sun had now disappeared in a slate-grey sky and a light wind had risen, lifting waste paper and empty cardboard cartons, the usual debris that was to be found on a building site. There was the sound of a distant siren from a tanker out in the bay, and the thud and hum of activity at the steel plant at Port Talbot came across to him on

131

the breeze. Henry stood quietly for a few minutes, listening to the sounds, and staring about him at the site. He thought back over the last few weeks and tried to remember the places where Jayo had led him in his ramblings, ostensibly searching for scaffolding equipment, but in reality seeking a place to hide from Geordie Banion.

Or so Henry had assumed.

He counted on his fingers. There were perhaps eight places that could be described as Jayo's favourite hiding-places – favourite, if one regarded the number of times Jayo visited them as being symptomatic of favour. Five of them were disused bunkers, none of them were in current use in the sense that gangs worked in them. Two were fairly near to Twll-Mawr, which lay in the centre of the site, but the others were more or less on the perimeter of the area. It was a point Henry had not considered before, but as he thought of it now he realized that the sites of Jayo's hideaways were all placed in a semi-circle that took in the west side of the building site. Its significance was not yet clear to him, but if he visited them now, perhaps he'd be able to think more clearly about the whole situation.

Henry waited until some shouting workmen had disappeared into Twll-Mawr, and then he set out to visit the first of the sites to which Jayo Davies was attracted. As he walked over the mounds of rubble and skirted the piles of con-crete blocks that littered the area, he wondered again what had happened to Jayo, for he had not been seen on the site since the time Tommy Bighead had died. Henry could guess where he

132

had gone, but it would be only a guess.

Henry climbed down into the first of the bunkers. It was quiet down there, and dim, the kind of sepulchral gloom that Jayo Davies liked as a haven from the demands of Geordie Banion. There was a pool of scummy water directly under the opening to the bunker and the concrete walls were damp. The floor was littered with rusting pieces of iron, and a few scaffolding clips were collected in a corner, no doubt as an excuse for Jayo to come down from time to time.

Henry wandered towards the far end of the bunker where it was darkest, but as his eyes grew used to the gloom he could see piles of rubble where part of the roof would seem to have fallen in. He turned, climbed back out of the bunker and emerged carefully, looking around him. There was no one in sight, but some hundred yards away the chimney of the site night-watchman, Young Beckie, had begun to smoke. He was on duty anyway.

Henry visited two more bunkers, not quite knowing what he was looking for or why, but one thing he did confirm to himself: all three formed part of the semi-circular perimeter of the site. He felt, somehow, there should be some significance in it, but for the time being it escaped him.

After the three bunkers there were two places that could be described as little more than holes in the ground. They had been excavated as foundations for plant to be bedded in, but when the scheme had folded they had been left as they were, to await a more sensible plan for the development of North Margam. They were perhaps eighty feet wide and broken up into sections, with concrete and steel joists forming an interlocking roof area that had been partly covered over to prevent accidents. There were several possible entrances and Jayo had used each of them in turn. Henry selected the nearest and dropped down into the darkness. Here, it really was dark, and his mouth was dry again as he thought of rats. Granda talked of rats in the pit in the old days, and though Henry had seen few at Margam he was always afraid that one of these days he might come face to face with a big one, all red eyes and sharp teeth.

He did not stay long in the holes.

The next stop was the bunker that Henry had spent some little time in before he had come up to see Phil Irish walking away towards the kilns. It was past the timber stack, near the hopper, and Henry kept a wary eye on Morris Weasel's office as he walked past it, just in case Morris was there and should ask him what he was up to. Henry decided not to bother going down into the bunker; he could give that one a miss. He walked on, heading for the next of Jayo's hideaways, but as he did so his step slowed. Something was beginning to click away in his brain. The bunker he had been in before he saw Phil had had something in common with at least one other of Jayo's secret places. Henry's step slowed, then stopped. He hesitated, the germ in his mind growing. He turned, walked back to the bunker behind the hopper and stood looking down into it.

After a moment he dropped down.

Under the darkening sky little light seemed to penetrate into the bunker. Henry stood there for a while and then hesitantly, with one hand out-stretched, he made his way towards the corner where he had been sitting on his previous visit. There was now no place where he could sit, and Henry stood there puzzled, and yet with the germ now beginning to flourish and grow strongly in his mind. He thought back to the other place, the other hideaway like this one, and he turned, re-traced his steps, grabbed the stanchions riveted into the wall and began to climb out of the bunker.

The wind had lifted, become gustier, and Henry saw a piece of newspaper fly past the opening above his head. He climbed up, reaching for the top stanchion with his left hand, releasing his grip with his right.

In that moment he saw the shoe. It moved forward swiftly. It kicked viciously at his fingers, graz-ing his knuckles sharply, and in spite of himself Henry reacted, letting go of the stanchion. For one moment he stood balanced, feet on the lower stanchions but unsupported by his hands, and then the shoe came forward again, shoving against his chest, and Henry went crashing backwards, down into the bunker.

He shouted loudly in surprise and anger, but the call was thumped out of him as he crashed heavily to the concrete floor of the bunker, winded. He lay there for several seconds, dazed, unbelieving, and he became aware that the little light from the opening above his head was blocked out as the man who had attacked him came scrambling down into the bunker. Henry tried to rise but he felt sick suddenly; he knelt there, watching the man as he reached the bottom and turned to face him, and an unreasoning fear arose in his throat as the man came closer. He struggled to rise from his knees but the man reached forward, grabbed his shirt collar, yanked him violently upwards, dragging him sideways into the semi-darkness of the bunker.

Then harsh and bright the torch-light stabbed at his eyes. He heard a grunt, and the grasp at his collar slackened. There was a certain disappointment in the voice when it came.

'Bloody hell! Henry Jones.'

CHAPTER IV

1

'Thought you was done for then, boy, didn't you?'

A match scratched, and when Detective-Superintendent Morgan drew on the cigarette he lit, Henry could see the sardonic amusement in his eyes. The policeman was squatting on his heels, not the way that miners did, squarely, but as rugby players did at half time, leaning sideways slightly, weight on one heel or the other, never both. Morgan seemed massive as he squatted there, his shoulders wide and hunched, his head low, thrust forward in menacing fashion. Henry, his back against the wall of the bunker, drew a nervous hand across his mouth.

'What ... what did you push me down like that for?' he asked.

'Didn't know it was you, did I?' Morgan replied amiably.

'You could cause a bad accident like that.'

'Didn't, though.'

'I could have broken my neck.'

'Only intended knockin' a bit of stuffin' out of you.' Morgan drew on his cigarette thoughtfully. 'Did too, didn't I?'

Henry's courage began to rise as his breath returned to normal. 'Why the hell did you do it, anyway?'

'No.' Morgan shook his head. 'I'm asking the questions. Get paid to do it, like. Already explained, haven't I, that I didn't know it was you down here. Thing is, what were *you* doin' down here? Shift's over, isn't it?'

'It's over.'

'So...?'

Henry was silent. It was not that he was unwilling to speak, but he was still angry at Morgan's treatment of him, and allied to that was the fact that his reasons for being in the bunker were only half formed – and he had no desire to put forward such theories as he had to a police detective-superintendent. So he remained silent, and the silence lengthened as Morgan's cigarette glowed in the semi-darkness.

'What's the trouble, son?' Morgan asked at length. When Henry still made no reply, he sighed. 'Bit angry, like, is it? Ah, well, no matter. Wanted to have a talk with you I did, anyway, and now and here is a good enough time and place.'

137

'Talk about what?'

'Questions I asked you before, but with a bit more meat on them, if you know what I mean.'

Henry swallowed hard. His throat felt sore, and his head was beginning to ache. 'I told you all I know, last time I saw you.'

'Maybe. But that presupposes I was asking all the right questions. And I learned long ago, in the front row, you got to keep on asking different questions, if you're goin' to screw the other chap down. Pose different problems, like a thumb in the eye, accidental, or teeth in his ear, fleshy part. That's how you make a man knuckle under, see. Show him who's boss. I just showed you who was boss, didn't I? Even if it wasn't you I expected to see here.'

'Who did you expect?' Henry asked snappishly.

'My questions, son, my questions. But I'll answer. One of a number of people. But not you. Because you're clever, isn't it, Henry? University education, like.'

Henry began to turn, preparatory to rising. The anger was sour in his throat and he had no desire to talk more with this violent, unpleasant policeman. The cigarette glowed again and the piggy eyes were still cruel and sardonic. 'Sit still, Henry Jones. I want you to tell me a few things.'

Henry sat back. There was something intensely and physically intimidating in Morgan's voice, and Henry's anger was not strong enough to withstand it. He leaned back, his head against the concrete. Morgan grunted contentedly. 'That's better, son, much better. Now relax. And listen for a moment.'

Gryfydd Morgan tapped a forefinger on his

138

cigarette to dislodge the ash and then looked about him. 'Lot of these on the site, isn't there? Funny place, North Margam. Nothing *controlled* about it. Whole operation is messy, seems to me, always has been. And maybe always will be, if the site has its way. All messy – except for one thing. You know what I'm talking about, Henry?'

Henry shook his head. Morgan grunted, shifted his weight to his other heel. 'Maybe, maybe not. We'll find out. But first I'd like you to go over what you told me the other day. About the way things went for you before Tommy Bighead got killed.'

'I already said–'

'I know,' Morgan interrupted soothingly. 'But let's clarify a few things, isn't it? Awright? Now then, first of all, in the course of the morning you saw several people.'

'As I always do.'

'Yes. But you saw more that morning because things seemed to be happening, wasn't that so?'

'I don't understand–'

'Oh, now, come on, you know all right. It was a funny morning, wasn't it? I mean, there was a kind of atmosphere, you said that to me.'

'It was just Monday morning. Always bad.'

'Washin' day, yes, but there was somethin' more on site,' Morgan insisted, an edge creeping into his tone. 'You said Tommy Bighead himself was more niggly than usual.'

'That's so. But–'

'All right, now who else did you see that morning?'

Henry considered. 'Mr Banion put me and Jayo Davies to work in Twll-Mawr. We didn't see any

139

others down there, but–'

'But–'

'Well,' Henry said awkwardly, 'Tonto Thomas called down to us at one point. He was looking for Phil Irish.'

'Right. Go on.'

Henry frowned, thinking hard. 'Jayo went off shortly after that – and I haven't seen him since. At break I joined ... no, I *went* to join the others but they weren't there. Until Mr Morris came across.'

'And what did he want?'

'He was looking for any of them – Tonto, Jayo or Phil. He went off. A bit later Tonto joined me, and so did Phil.'

'And how was *their* relationship?'

'As usual,' Henry lied, 'except for Monday morning feeling.'

'And you didn't see Tommy Bighead that morning, after you arrived on site?'

'No,' Henry lied again. 'Not till I saw him dead.'

'Hmmm...' Morgan was silent for a little while and Henry sweated. He had the feeling that Morgan knew he had lied in some detail and he dreaded a cross-examination on the matter. But it did not come. Instead, the detective-superintendent asked, 'Why were you climbing the scaffolding, Henry?'

Henry explained. Jayo had gone, Henry was afraid Banion might catch him, when Jayo did not return Henry thought he might be up on the roof, so he had begun to climb.

'He wasn't up there?'

'I saw no one. The roofers–'

'The roofers had been moved elsewhere for the morning,' Morgan said. 'But you saw no one up there. No one at all?'

Henry shook his head. 'The joist falling, it came as a shock to me. I felt the wind of its passing, and then I looked down–'

'Yes... And when you got down there was quite a group of them there, pulling away the wreckage. Tonto Thomas? Phil Irish? Banion? Jayo Davies?'

Henry's mouth was dry again. 'Only Banion. I saw him stagger with surprise when he realized there was a man in the shed. The others ... they must have been working elsewhere.'

'Up above?' Morgan asked casually.

'I wouldn't know.'

'Well, I'll tell you what *I* know, Henry Jones,' Morgan said coldly. 'I'm no fool. I got a long experience as a copper, and I got a nose. I'll tell you, when I was with the Cwmavon front row there was always a time when you could *tell*, as a matter of instinct, that things were happening. The very moment you got your opponent screwed down, you could tell. Ask any rugby player and he'll say the same; there's a moment in the game when you can smell victory – personal or team victory, you can smell it. I *always* knew when I'd ground down my man. Not by what he said or threatened or did – there was just an atmosphere, boy, I tell you. And it's the same in police work. There's a time when you can smell a problem even though you can't see it. Tommy Bighead was murdered, all right, and we got to find out why and by whom, but I got the feeling it was all tied up with something that happened that morning. You won't admit it, and the others is cagey too, but something did happen that day, and there was a funny kind of nigglin' going on, and I mean to find out what it was all about. Because I think it will tell me who killed Tommy Bighead. And there's another smell around too – maybe the same one, or connected with it. *Corruption.*'

Henry said nothing, and after a few moments the policeman chuckled. 'But you smell it too, don't you, Henry?'

'I don't know what you mean.'

'Then what you doin' down here, then?'

Henry was silent. Morgan waited, and the silence grew between them, became painful in its intensity. The cigarette died as Morgan waited. 'You was looking for something, wasn't that it, Henry?'

'Such as what?'

'You tell me.'

'I don't know,' Henry said miserably. 'It's just that–'

'Go on.'

Henry shook his head. His suspicions could be unfounded. 'Have you interviewed Jayo Davies yet?' he asked.

'James Olliphant Davies...' There was a smile in Morgan's voice. 'With a name like that no wonder he called himself Jayo. Wouldn't admit it to anyone. No ... haven't seen James Olliphant yet. Seems to have skipped, he does. And he didn't exactly like our dead friend, did he?'

'There was nothing to that,' Henry said hurriedly. 'A bit of fooling by Tommy Bighead–'

'Fibreglass, I heard,' Morgan interrupted.

142

'Nasty. Still, they all suffered from Tommy Big-head some time, didn't they? Tonto Thomas always bein' needled, Jayo, Phil Irish ... not you, though, Henry.'

'I explained that,' Henry said.

'Haven't explained what you're doin' down here. Well, all right, I'll give you a bit of help, like. You know Young Beckie?'

'The night-watchman. Yes, I know him.'

Morgan shook his head, ruefully admiring a vision of long ago. 'Saw him when I was a young-ster, you know. Bloody great, he was! Just five feet two and built like a lath, seemed to have no muscle on him, but he could move like a wisp of wind, and he snapped his punches from his shoulder in a way that used to rock a man's head so it seemed about to break free. Started in the boxing booths in Tonypandy, you know, where it was really rough, and he made it late in the pro-fessional ring. Could have been world champion but for that, they say. But there he is now – night-watchman, pot-bellied, grotesque.' He glanced up to Henry, dispelling memories and concen-trating on the present. 'Grotesque, and almost deaf, and more than a little punch drunk. Act of charity, it is, givin' him a job as night-watchman on the site. Charity – or somethin' else.'

'Something else?'

'You know what I mean, Henry. It's why you're down here.'

'I–'

'There's lorry tracks up above, even though there's no reason for lorries to run past here right now. *Fresh* lorry tracks. And there's money floating around the site – some of it found its way into Tommy Bighead's pocket. And the night-watchman's almost deaf and certainly *twp*. All adds up to something. And when I start sniffin' around the bunkers and see someone down this one, when he shouldn't be, it's just another nail in a coffin. Know what I mean, Henry?'

Henry's head was aching and his mind was a confused welter of puzzled anxieties. 'There were boxes,' he said. 'I sat on them only on Tuesday. But they're gone now.'

'Ahhh...' Morgan rocked on his heels thoughtfully. 'That's why you came down. Suspicious, like.'

'I knew there was something going on. No one is saying anything, but there's a tension, everyone's worried – and then I remembered that a couple of times, when I was with Jayo, I noticed crates, boxes, that sort of thing, stacked in dark corners of bunkers; meant nothing to me then, but here in this bunker...'

'You're a smart lad, Henry Jones.'

'I don't know what it all means.'

'But you're beginning to guess, as I was starting to guess,' Morgan said smugly. 'Bit of thievin', isn't it?'

Brenda had said it. That was how Henry's mind had switched to this track. She had planted the idea, the tension on the site had encouraged it, the memory of boxes in the bunker had brought it to flower.

'Happens on all sites,' Morgan said. 'Always a little bit of it goin' on. But if they're usin' lorries here, it's bigger, more regular, more organized.

So we don't want to go jumpin' too soon, do we, Henry? Thing is, to go careful. You understand? First, get all the little fish into the net, catch them all wriggling, and then haul in the big ones as well, the *organizers*. And then we can settle for Tommy Bighead as well.'

Henry stared at Morgan uncomprehendingly. 'Tommy Bighead?'

'Aw, come on, Henry, you're not forgetting the *big* thing in all this? I don't normally go around on building sites checkin' on fiddles! But murder is a different thing. That's why I'm here now. Because it's getting more and more clear to me now that there is a fiddle of some sort being worked on this site, and Tommy Bighead was involved in it, and somehow, somewhere, the wheel was coming off – and I think it came off on Monday morning. And *that* was why Tommy Bighead died. Not because he was unpopular. Not because he scratched Jayo Davies with fibreglass, and put dog turds in Tonto Thomas's tommybox, and needled Phil Irish, and baited half the other men on the site. He had a hundred and fifty quid in his pocket and my guess is it came from a fiddle on the site – and because something blew on Monday morning Tommy Bighead died!' He stood up, stretching. He flicked the torch on again, shone it around the empty bunker. 'You'll want to be getting home. I'll give you a lift down to the station.'

They drove down into Port Talbot. Henry felt sick and dazed. He could not seize upon any logical thought; his mind was confused with resentments and denials and old loyalties and friendships. His suspicions had, it seemed, been confirmed; Gryfydd Morgan was working along the same lines as Henry had guessed. But Henry was one step ahead of the detective-superintendent. He knew the identities of the men involved in the fiddle.

Morgan sat behind the wheel of the car, big, heavy, his piggy eyes never still, his great ham hands gripping the steering wheel tightly. He was in a chatty expansive mood as he drove Henry towards the station, but suddenly Henry knew he didn't want to go home. It was important that he see Phil Irish. He had to talk it out with him; he owed him that much at least, as a friend. And he could not believe that Phil Irish could have been involved in the death of Tommy Bighead.

'I won't be able to get a train home for a couple of hours,' Henry blurted, as they drove through the middle of town. 'I think I'll go get a drink or something; a sandwich, maybe.'

'All right, Henry, where shall I drop you?'

'Across there will do,' Henry said hurriedly. The car slowed, Morgan drew the vehicle in towards the kerb, and across the street the neon lights above The Brick Wall were already shining. Morgan glanced casually across to the sign – ARFON'S – and then put one massive hand on Henry's arm just as he was about to get out of the car.

'A word, Henry.'

'Yes?'

Morgan smiled. It was a vast, toothy, insincere smile that held edges of menace. 'Took you into

146

my confidence a bit, Henry, but I did it for a reason. You're sharp; clever. University education. And you know a few men on the site. They talk. Chat. Say things in unguarded moments. Won't say things like that to a copper who questions them. But off guard they'll be, when you're around them. So I'll tell you what I want. I want you to do a bit of listening for me. And anything you hear, I want you to bring to me. Understand?'

Henry sat stiffly in the seat. 'You want me to spy for you, Mr Morgan.'

'Griff,' the detective said soothingly. 'Call me Griff, like my other friends. And the word *spy* – that's harsh, that is. Informer is better.'

'I'm no–'

'Now hold on, boyo. Don't get carried away. Let's face facts. I didn't ask you to go down that bunker. You went down yourself, because you *wanted* to poke your nose in. So now I'm asking you to poke your nose in. Not deep; just to keep me informed if anything odd comes up in general chat.'

'It's a dirty business.'

'You want to play front row in a scrum some time, boyo. Now *that's* dirty. Informing – just necessary, that is. Part of the business. Business of every civic-minded citizen. I mean, if something criminal comes to your attention, you don't hide it from the police, do you? Law abiding, you are. So ... help us out, when you can. That's all. I got confidence in you, see, because you got brains. Use brains, I can. So if you pick anything up, let me know, isn't it? Make your people back home in the Rhondda proud it would, to know you're helping

147

the police under cover. You can tell them later, when it's all over. Girls would be after you then, for sure.'

Brenda. A surge of fury swept over Henry, and he moved away from Morgan's restraining hand.

'Aye, well,' Morgan said, and glanced towards the neon sign with a knowing grin. 'In the meantime, have a good time. See you on site, whenever.'

He was still sitting there in the car when Henry plucked up courage to go through the doors beneath the neon sign.

2

There was a precious young man in a dinner-jacket and black tie standing just inside the doors, and he looked Henry up and down as though he had seen valley sheep root better things out of dustbins.

'Labour Club's next block, boy,' he said and flicked the ruffles on his mauve shirt.

'I'm not coming in,' Henry said, trying to peer past the elegant little man.

'Bloody right you're not. Dressed like a bloody brickie. Bit of class in here it is, not for *mochyns* like you.'

Henry looked at him and something in his glance took much of the bravura out of the mauve-shirted man's tone. 'What are you lookin' for anyway?' he asked, less belligerently.

'Is Helen Swain still here?'

'Aye. Just packin' up, she is. Why?'

'I want to see her.'

Mauve-shirt sniffed, stepped back a pace and looked Henry up and down, then shrugged. 'I'll tell her, if you like, long as you stay out there on the pavement. Won't do our trade any good, havin' you standin' there. Make us look like a roadside caff.'

Henry stepped out to the pavement outside. The sky was leaden, heavy clouds piling up, and the breeze sent leaves scurrying along the street as he waited. He looked at his watch; it was gone half past six. Maybe he could get a train back about eight. He heard a step behind him and he turned to see Helen Swain coming out of the night-club, shrugging into her topcoat, smiling faintly as she recognized him, crinkling her nose like a child.

'Hello, Henry. Waiting for me, is it?' Perhaps in spite of herself there was a certain teasing invitation in her tone, and it made Henry vaguely uneasy.

'I was just wondering if you'd know whether Phil would be down tonight.'

'Phil?' She looked slightly puzzled. 'Well, *bach*, you work with him, you ought to know where he'd go. Back to his digs, I suppose. You tried there?'

'Well ... no.' Henry shuffled his feet. 'I got a lift down the town, and got off over there and saw the club well, I just wondered if Phil—'

'Haven't seen that Irish mick since last weekend,' Helen said, buttoning her coat. 'Saturday afternoon he went off to put a bet on and he's not been around since. Typical. Didn't even thank me for pulling him out of that alley.' She hesitated, then glanced sharply at Henry. 'Missed your train again, then?'

'Something like that. I'll get one in an hour or so. I just thought that maybe Phil–'

'To hell with Phil. Come on, you can buy me a drink. It's been a long day and I'm cheesed off with that damned Arfon Rhayader.' She linked her arm into his and half turned him away from the club, towards the pub at the corner of the street. Henry was hardly aware of the movement because something she had said struck a responsive chord in his mind, yet he could not understand what it was. A vague unpleasant memory touched him, like a cobweb on his face in the darkness, but then it was gone as she said again, 'I said, you don't object to buying me a drink, do you?'

'Eh? Oh no, of course not.'

'In here, then.'

They turned into the pub. As Henry hesitated, she steered him through the left-hand door and into the public bar. She told him she'd be happy with a gin and tonic, and as she settled herself in the seat under the window Henry went up to the bar, ordered her drink and a lager for himself. When he went across to join her she moved, shuffling sideways.

'There you are, you can have the warm place.' She picked up her drink, sipped it, and sighed. 'Thanks. Needed this, I did. It's been a mucky day.'

'Never mind. Finishing soon, aren't you?'

She pulled a face. 'Ah, well, that may be so, or it may not.'

'But Rhayader sacked you, gave you a week's

notice last Friday night, after Phil got fighting in the club. Didn't he mean what he said?'

Helen sipped her drink again and shrugged. 'He meant it all right. But he was pretty mad just then. And he's cooled off a bit, I suppose. He's spent most of today trying to persuade me to stay on after all. And get me to bed, of course.'

'You said he fancied you.'

'Oh, aye, and he also said last Friday that he was off that kick, remember?' She laughed, and her face lit up in a way Brenda's had not for a long time. 'I think for Arfon Rhayader that there must be a link between sex and business, though, you see.'

'How do you mean?'

'Well, when he's had a deal going and it's come up for him, it's a success that boosts his sex drive. So maybe he's pulled something this week, and that makes him put Phil into perspective and me into his sights again. So I guess, anyway.'

Henry frowned, not quite following the drift of her conversation. 'What sort of business are you talking about?'

The little laugh lines around Helen's eyes faded away and she grew serious, her plump, warm face becoming harder as she gazed thoughtfully at Henry. There was something calculating in her glance as though she was trying to weigh him up, reach a decision of some kind. She shrugged. 'Business ... well, there's all sorts of business gets done in a club like Arfon's, and if a girl's got any common sense and keeps her eyes open she begins to pick up a few ideas. I don't know, maybe that's why Arfon is being friendly again. Perhaps he wouldn't want us to part on *too* unfriendly terms, in case I ended up more angry than scared.'

Henry shook his head. 'Really, I don't know what you're talking about.'

Helen leaned forward, her voice taking on a mock serious note, a wise mother talking to her innocent son. 'Well, I'll spell it out for you, then, for we can't have Henry running around without knowing his head from his backside, can we? Let me put it like this. A night-club like Arfon Rhayader's, it sails close to the wind. All sorts of blokes come in, and some of them have got a hell of a lot of money. No one asks where they got it from, as long as they spend it in the club; but some of them don't come to spend money, they come to work out how to *make* it.'

'Businessmen?'

'You could call them that,' Helen replied with a grin. 'They certainly come in to do business, that's for sure. But it's a bit of under-the-counter stuff, you know? For instance, I know from the books that Arfon sells a hell of a lot more liquor than he buys legitimately. So where does he get his stocks from? Off the back of a lorry, I suppose. And he's got a lot more of that kind of thing going that I know nothing about. Graft all over the place. That's why he got the club in the first place, isn't it, and that's how he'll be a millionaire in the end. Non-taxable profits.'

'And you know about some of his criminal activities?' Henry asked, frowning. He was thinking of Brenda, and how furious she would be if she could see him now, talking of such matters with a woman who worked – albeit as a cashier –

in a night-club.

'Some of the petty stuff,' Helen said. 'But not much detail. But you never know, do you? I mean, suppose the police was to ask me, and I gave them some little bit of information that wasn't very important in itself, but was a link in a chain of evidence, like. Could put the skids under Arfon Rhayader, couldn't I? Oh, I could tell a few little tales out of school about Arfon – about his rake-off on the bookies, for instance – but no detail. Could say a few things about some of the surprisingly prominent local people who come into the club to see him too. And that's why Arfon wouldn't want us to part *really* bad friends.'

'In case you got more angry than scared,' Henry said thoughtfully.

'That's right. Arfon knows that *I* know if I was to start saying things to the wrong people I could end up getting scarred. And that's enough to shut me up. But if we was to get really angry with each other, and I got shirty, I might say something damaging in spite of the threat.'

She sipped her gin and Henry stared at her wide-eyed, marvelling that she could talk so calmly about such matters, things that seemed to him to belong more to a London or Chicago gangland than to a Welsh steel town. She caught his glance, and smiled. 'Aw, come on. Exaggeratin' a bit, I was, that's all. Trying to impress you. I don't really know very much about Arfon Rhayader – only that he is a bit of a crook, that's all. And that he gets around West Wales a bit. But it's none of my business, is it?'

Henry sighed. 'No, I suppose not.'

'Besides, it's Phil you want to talk about, not Arfon Rhayader.'

'Phil?' Henry glanced at her cautiously. 'I want to see him, not talk about him. I just thought he might be meeting you this evening and–'

'Like I said,' she interrupted him, shaking her head, 'haven't seen him since Saturday. It's been a funny time, I tell you. First, the brawl in The Brick Wall, then after you crept out in the morning before we were awake, Phil and I, well, *we* had a quarrel. Maybe he had a hangover, or perhaps he was mad because he got kicked by Arfon's boys a bit, I don't know, but suddenly we were playing war with each other.'

'What was it about?' Henry asked.

'Me, I suppose,' she said, suddenly glum. 'Oh, hell, there's times I get depressed, you know; life just hasn't played fair, seems to me sometimes – I mean, I've had more than my share of trouble. My husband ... well, anyway, we got talking about the past and about the future and somehow it turned into a quarrel. I mean, Phil wanted to dig, know more than he needed to about how things have been for me, and it wasn't his business. So in the end he stormed off. Haven't seen him since. He'll be back, though – maybe tonight. What did you want to see him about, anyway?'

Henry shrugged. He didn't really want to tell her, and yet in an odd way he did want to speak about it, if only to test out his anxieties on someone else. He hesitated, but she pressed him, her natural curiosity being underpinned by her regard for Phil Irish, and Henry began to talk, to explain his half-formed theories, the guesses he was

154

making, unsupported by real evidence. She made him backtrack a couple of times as he became confused, and cloaked his meaning with refusals to name names. But over the course of the next hour she got most of his worries out of him, and bought two drinks to his one in the process.

'All right,' she said at the end quietly, 'so what does it all boil down to? You think that Phil is mixed up some way in Tommy Bighead's murder.'

'I didn't exactly *say* that.'

'No, but you're saying a lot of things that lead towards that, if you ask me. To start with you're suggesting that there's a gang on site working some sort of fiddle that the police are on to, and maybe Phil is one of that gang. Tommy Bighead was also involved, and as a result of something that happened on Monday morning Tommy Bighead was killed. With money in his pocket. And you think Phil threw that concrete joist down on the little man?'

'I didn't *say* that! I just wanted ... I just thought if I could have a talk with Phil ... warn him about Detective-Superintendent Morgan ... look, Helen, maybe if Phil would talk to me, tell me what it's all about, it would be clear to me he's not involved and I'd be easier in my mind, and wouldn't have to...' He was on the point of saying he wouldn't have to worry about informing to Gryfydd Morgan to the same extent, but he bit back the words. When he looked at Helen he wasn't sure that she was even aware of his hesitation, however. Her eyes were clouded, and she was thinking hard, a deep line appearing between her brows.

'Phil couldn't...' Her glance cleared and she

looked sharply at Henry. 'Just because he gets fighting mad from time to time, it doesn't mean Phil could have–'

'I *know*. Besides, there are others who disliked Tommy Bighead enough to kill him, maybe. I mean, he was always needling Tonto Thomas, and Jayo Davies hasn't even been seen since the killing.'

'But you still want to talk it out with Phil.' When Henry shrugged mournfully, she put down her glass abruptly. 'All right then, you'd better take me home.'

She was silent in the bus, after explaining to him that it was possible Phil would turn up there that evening. At seven-thirty in the evening he certainly wouldn't be at his own digs.

Her flat was only a short walk from the bus stop and he followed her sheepishly, and a little drunk again, though nowhere near as intoxicated as he had been on the previous Friday. She climbed the stairs ahead of him and unlocked the door. She went in, called out aloud and then returned to the door. 'No. Phil's not here.' She hesitated, staring at Henry undecidedly. 'What time is your train?'

'Eight-fifteen. Half eight. I'm not sure. It doesn't matter, though.'

'Come on. You better come in for a while. Chance is Phil could turn up in the next fifteen minutes and you'll have just missed him then, wouldn't you?'

Henry followed her into the flat, closing the door behind him.

'Got his own key, he has,' Helen said, half grumbling. 'So he can come and go as he pleases.

Treats me like he owns me, it's not right. Too damned happy-go-lucky, he is, doesn't know when he's well off. Siddown, Henry, while I go and get changed.'

Henry sat down. He put his head against the chairback. Suddenly he felt extremely miserable. Perhaps it was because he had had a few drinks again, but as depression washed over him he suddenly asked himself what the hell was going on. What was he doing here in Helen Swain's flat? For that matter he had no idea any more what he was doing at North Margam or why he was so concerned about Phil Irish. The man was only a casual workmate; Henry owed him nothing; they were not particularly close friends. And yet Henry had lied to a detective-superintendent to cover up for Phil Irish, and now he was seeking him out, to obtain an explanation from him before he was called upon to give further details to Gryfydd Morgan. But why did Henry feel such a responsibility to Phil Irish? Maybe it was nothing more than that man Morgan's attitude that caused it. Henry resented his using him as an *informer*. Perhaps Henry was just getting back at Morgan, expiating some of the personal guilt he felt at even talking to the policeman about workmates.

Or maybe it was more than that. Maybe it was the stain of a slow suspicion, a whisper in the brick kilns, Phil Irish disappearing into the kilns, another man, a whisper ... and what was it that Helen had *said...?* There had been something, a word, an inflection, and it fluttered around in his mind just out of reach, intangible and incomprehensible.

'What's the matter with you?'

157

Henry opened his eyes and raised his head from the chairback. Helen was coming in from the bedroom, and she had changed into a loose skirt and a baggy sweater. She looked more casual and strangely enough more attractive to Henry; younger, more vulnerable, softer in frame and in appearance. She looked more like the image he had seen in that old faded photograph of her wedding day, a young girl standing beside that tall awkward man, and something seemed to move in Henry's chest, as a warmth stole over him, a feeling of almost protective tenderness.

'Are you all right?' Helen asked suspiciously.

When Henry nodded she walked across to the Welsh dresser that stood, darkly incongruous, in the corner of the room. She took out a bottle of whisky and poured herself a drink. Almost absent-mindedly she handed one to Henry also, and then she crossed to the other easy chair and sat down, with her legs curled up under her. He frowned as she sipped at her undiluted whisky.

'You think Phil really *is* mixed up in something serious?'

'I don't know,' Henry said unhappily. 'The fact is, I don't seem to know anything these days.'

'What's that supposed to mean?'

A maudlin self-pity swept over Henry as he stared at the drink he held in his hands. He almost felt like crying. 'Don't you ever get the feeling that everything's going wrong, that life's soured, there's something you ought to be doing about it but can't, and your whole existence is just one big mess?'

Her eyes fell away from his. 'I know the feeling

exactly, Henry. Exactly.'

'Well, that's how things are for me. I just don't know where I'm going, Helen. No idea.'

She looked up again after a moment, watched him feeling sorry for himself. 'Just what *are* you doing at Margam, Henry?'

Perhaps it was because she was older than he; it might have been because she was almost a stranger to him; possibly it was on account of the softness of her voice, the fact that she was a woman, the fact that even though uninvolved with him she wanted to know. So where he was unable to find the words with Brenda, or his grandfather, or Nan, he could tell Helen Swain, talk to her, attempt to explain, but as much to himself as to her.

'I've been asking myself the same question ever since I started,' he said. 'And yet, before I started, it seemed clear enough. Somewhere along the way it's got all confused, in a way I can't fathom... You see, it's like it's all to do with hopes and expectations. Here I am – a graduate. Certain things are expected of me. *I* expect certain things. You know what it's like to win a degree at university? Anticlimax, that's what it's like. Big build-up, then nothing. But people think you're different; proud of you, they are. They don't realize that inside, maybe only for a while, something's died. Expectations, maybe. You *expect* something from getting a degree. I got nothing. Fell flat, it did, completely flat.'

'I don't see–'

'But there's more to it than that, as well. It all goes back much further. I worked hard for my degree, and it was just sawdust in the end. And I

159

came back to the valley and the family looked at me like I was God. And had expectations. I just couldn't do what they wanted – that was it. Because ... well, in the end you got to ask yourself what it's all about.'

'What *what's* all about?'

'Look, take my grandfather, for instance.' Henry leaned forward earnestly in his chair, hands together, fingers intertwined, and it was almost as though he was in a seminar room again, conducting a philosophical argument, pursuing it to its ineffectual conclusion. 'As a young man, he was in the pits, and the wrong sack of flour got delivered to the house. Inside was a leg of ham. Knock on the door; man saying he'd delivered wrong sack. Whose sack was it, then? Gwylym Elias – chairman of the Co-op Stores Committee. My grandfather, at that point, saw what he wanted out of life. He had an aim – to become chairman of the Stores Committee in the Co-op.'

'I'm sure you're making a point, but–'

'He *achieved* that aim, so in a sense his life has not been wasted. Set himself a clear goal, and reached it. But how was it achieved, and why was it achieved? I'll tell you – by hard work – and by bribery. He got there by giving favours and once he was there he received them. And that's what life is all about, you see. Giving favours. And more than favours – money, gifts, backhanders, bribes. It's corruption, that's what it's all about. Corruption. And am I any different?'

Helen's face had softened. She stared at him, her lips parted slightly. 'You obviously don't think so,' she said.

'I'm no different at all. My old man gave me the gift of his life; he worked in the pits when I was young and died there because we needed money. My mother died when I was twelve, so what do I owe her? My grandparents gave me love and a home, and they tried to embroil me in the kind of love the valley has for all its sons and I took it and accepted it, and I knew that one day I would gain power and local eminence and prestige. But what would it all be built on? *Favours*. A *giving* – and then a grabbing back. It's a market place, see, a place where people buy and sell people. I can't live my own life; I'm shackled to what the valley has preordained for me. Even the State's no different – I get a grant to go to university, and what's that but a payment to make me do something later that repays the State? They buy you, buy your brain, twist your views, tear out the last independent gut you possess, force you into a mould that suits them, and the society you live in. It's buying all the time, and the setting of worthless goals. And I don't want it. So I opted out of it. I refused to do what they wanted. And I came to Margam.'

'But what do you gain by taking a job on the building site?'

Henry frowned. It was a question that had puzzled him much of late. He shook his head. 'It was a matter of principle at first. I wanted to do something ... that was useful, productive, like. And I wanted time ... time to think. And I wanted to show them, make them see, and there was Brenda...'

'Ah.' Helen was smiling faintly, one eyebrow raised in mockery. 'So there's a girl in it too.'

Henry shrugged. 'She's no different. She's even worse than the rest, in a way. I mean, she says she loves me, but she's buying too – buying me with the promise of her body. But all she thinks of is marriage – nothing beyond that. No matter to her if I stifle in a white collar job, lose my self-respect by creeping around councillors, not as long as she gets a wedding ring on her finger and a respectable man for a husband. That's her aim in life – in a way, as simple as my grandfather's. And just as ... meaningless.'

'We all have to have an aim, Henry.' Helen's eyes had misted slightly, as though his words made her sad. 'And your girl ... well, I understand her feelings. I can tell you, there was a time when I thought a man, and marriage, could solve all sorts of problems.'

'All right,' Henry agreed, 'you told me, you wanted to get out of Bute Street so you went with a man, and he was possessive and you tried to solve that by marrying him. But can't you see the difference? Those were short-term aims – like my aims here at Margam. But Brenda – she's *got* no other aims and never will. And if I give in, if I adopt the standards and the myopic viewpoints of people in the valley, what the hell is life for?'

Helen snorted cynically. 'Short term, long term, what's the difference, really? Henry, let me tell you, if you don't have a clear aim, you can end up with never having any achievements at all.'

Henry shook his head emphatically. 'I can't agree with that. My grandfather, he saw it like a distant flag, a banner to reach for. I can't see any such point to aim for – nothing that's worthwhile,

162

anyway. They want me to conform to a way of life I've grown away from – damn, six months out of the valley and a man begins to change, but they can't see it.'

'Are you sure you've changed, Henry? Or is it that you just *want* to change?' Helen took another sip of her whisky, rose and came across to perch on the arm of Henry's chair. She looked down at him, smiling again, but her smile held a hint of sad reflection. 'I envy your grandfather, and *you* ought to. At least he saw what he wanted, reached for it, and got it. I reached too, but it failed me sadly. You – you be careful, Henry. You could drift. You could be on a sea and go nowhere in the darkness. Take another look at your valley. Ask yourself if things have really changed for you. Take another look at your girl – and ask yourself whether maybe you're the one who's wrong, not her. But don't just opt out, because I tell you, there's nothing to be gained by running away.' Something happened to Helen's eyes at that moment, as though the shadow of a painful memory passed over them. 'Nothing at all,' she added after a moment. 'I *know*.'

'I can't accept the valley any more.'

'Got to tie yourself to something, you have. Can't stay loose. Either you find your values in the valley, or outside. But I tell you this, Henry – you won't find them by running to Margam and the building site. That way, you'll just get torn.'

'The way *you* did?'

She looked at him quietly for a moment, and then nodded. She leaned against the back of his chair, her arm raised to steady her, and he was aware of the outline of her breast under the sweater and the warmth of her body leaning unselfconsciously over him. 'Yes,' she said, 'the way I did. At sixteen it was an escape; at eighteen it was a fading hope, and at nineteen it was a bloody prison. There was just no way, Henry, no way in which I could find peace. You'll never know what it's like to be subjected to the kind of nagging persistent jealousy that I suffered from my husband. I didn't need to do anything, say anything, speak to or even look at anyone. It was all a state of mind. I tell you, we could be at home, sitting in a room together, and I'd suddenly catch him watching me and there'd be a look of ... well, it was like *loathing* on his face. And I knew what he was thinking. There'd be worms in his mind about the past, about the old days when he pulled me out of Bute Street and I went willingly to his bed because it was an escape, but there'd be worms in the *present* too because he couldn't accept that I was faithful to him. If it was like that when we were alone together, it was worse when I was out. If another man looked at me, and I wasn't even aware of it, he'd still insist that I'd led the bloke on. When I went shopping alone I always had the feeling that he was behind me somewhere, watching me, checking on me. In the end, he did just that; he got to the pitch that he wouldn't let me out of his sight.'

She looked down at Henry, with a strange sadness in her eyes. 'It wore me down. I lost weight, got listless, desperate at times, crying nights. But funny enough, the worst thing was the way it affected him. I mean, he *had* me, didn't he? We was *living* together. But it wasn't enough. He began to look ill and drawn. I guessed it was insecurity and he needed to feel that I was really his; security lay in his *owning* me. So I married him.'

'But it didn't help,' Henry said.

'It didn't help. Things got worse, in fact. I began to feel hemmed in. I liked a good time. I was just a kid. But every time I suggested we went out there was a row. We ended up fighting most of the time. And he began to change. Even more, I mean. Obsession, it was. He started missing shifts. He'd say he was going, then he wouldn't go. Or he'd come back unexpectedly in the middle of the day, and if I was out shopping he'd come spyin' on me. Sometimes he'd pretend to go to work, and then hide around the corner, in the paper shop, anywhere. Just tryin' to catch me out all the time. He never got any satisfaction out of it; never caught me at anything. And in a sense that was worse.'

'How do you mean?'

'Well, if he'd caught me with another man he could have spilled his obsession out, maybe. I mean, he had this thing that I was dirty, that I was cheating on him, that I was the whore he'd found in Bute Street. He had no proof – and he had no *justification* for his conduct. And it was killing him. Where he'd been a big, handsome feller he'd lost weight. His face got all drawn, lines along here, see? He got grim, rarely talked, never smiled. He was just looking for trouble. All the time.' She finished her drink. 'So, in the end, when I couldn't stand it no more, I left him.'

'Did he come after you?' Henry asked.

'Oh aye. Chased all over...' Helen hesitated,

seemed about to add something more, then thought better of it. 'So there you are, Henry, we all have our problems. But you, you're just running away. Not like I did. I took a decision. You're avoiding one. You got to commit yourself in the end. Got to *decide*, you have. Decisions can raise more problems than you're facing, and it takes courage to take a decision, but you can't just go on hoping. Got to act, you have. And when you commit yourself, follow it through.' She smiled. 'Now then, what about your train?'

Henry shrugged. 'Missed it, I expect, by now. And Phil might yet come. If you don't mind, I'll hang on a bit.'

'I don't mind.' Helen rested her cheek on her hand. She suddenly looked very young. 'When you were talking before, it sounded ... I don't know. I liked to hear it. Made me feel ... motherly. Don't know any man who's made me feel that.'

'Doesn't sound complimentary,' Henry said thickly.

'Oh, it is,' she said, and her eyes were bright. There was a thumping in Henry's chest as he looked at her, and he was more than ever conscious of her nearness. Unbidden, the memory of that photograph in the bedroom came again and there was something of her young face above him now and he wanted to reach up and touch it. He could not explain his feelings and perhaps it was just the whisky heating his blood, but he wanted to be close to her. Perhaps it was because he felt sympathy for her or because he felt he had achieved a certain intimacy with her, in the course of this short period in her flat, that had been lacking in all

166

his previous relationships. He had talked to her, unburdened himself in a way he hadn't found possible with his grandparents, or with Brenda. It created a bond between them, an emotional bond that was heightened by the warm curves of her body above him, the brightness of her eyes as she looked back to an unhappy youth, and he reached up and touched her face with his hand.

Her reaction surprised him, and made the thumping in his chest even louder. She half turned her face, cradled it into his hand, and her eyes began to close. She looked even younger, her face seemed to shine and glow, and it was as though Henry was observing a transformation, a reaching back to lost years, and he was profoundly moved by the thought. He craned upwards, and he kissed her.

She responded as though she were in a dream. He had the impression that she did not know where she was; he felt that she was a million mental miles from him, but it didn't matter, for something told him that it was all unreal anyway. The soft wetness of her mouth was real, the warmth of her body as she slid down on to the chair with him, that was real enough, but it was as though they were both acting out some private dream for each other, dissociated from reality, slipping into a phantom world where they could escape the harsh facts of their existence. They kissed, and they clung to each other, and when Henry slipped his hand beneath her sweater, he realized she wore nothing underneath it.

She opened her eyes and drew away from him. There was a slight alarm in her glance. 'Henry,' she said, as though recognizing him for the first time. 'This is silly.'

'He was a bloody fool,' Henry said.

'Who?'

'Swain.'

'Swain?'

'Your husband. Bloody fool, losing you that way. Making life impossible.'

'He couldn't help it,' she said, and smiled faintly. 'And *my* name's Swain – maiden name, that is. Wasn't *his* name. But if he could see me now, he'd say he'd been right all along, wouldn't he?'

Wrong as hell, Henry thought. Because this was different. They were like two lost souls, Henry and Helen, finding a brief haven in each other. Helen and her wasted unhappy years, Henry and his stumbling, blundering present, full of anxieties and irresolution, asking questions and finding no answers. For a little while perhaps they could both find peace in each other, and though she resisted, struggling slightly, he kissed her again, until the resistance melted and there was a funny sound deep in her throat and he knew she felt the way he did. Not committed, not even loving, but fulfilling a need that existed, and could be satisfied for a little while.

Then someone shouted like an enraged bull.

Helen's eyes came wide open and she tore her mouth away from his, so that he saw a tiny trickle of saliva at the corner of her lips. There was sheer panic in her face, and yet it was not a present panic, it was rooted in a fearful past, and she was pushing Henry away, trying to scramble from his lap. In the event it was unnecessary. A large, familiar grip took Henry by the collar and dragged him backward out of the chair, and a furious, convulsed face was above him, glaring down as he twisted and tried to rise. The mouth was open, snarling, and then the violent eyes snapped away from him to Helen Swain.

'*You stupid whore!*' Phil Irish bawled. 'Don't you ever learn?'

She had backed away against the wall. Her hair was untidy and one ineffectual hand was up, plucking at it, the other crammed, childlike, against her frightened mouth. Her eyes were wide and staring, glazed with terror, as though she was looking at something almost nameless, half forgotten, dredged from the years of her childhood and her youth. Henry had the fleeting impression that the unreality of the last few minutes remained with Helen – all this was unreal too, the violence and the shouting and the hysterical, jealous rage. But it was real enough for Henry. The knuckles of the Irishman's fist dug into his neck and he felt his own temper rising, fanned by whisky and guilt. He grabbed at Phil Irish's wrist, tried to tear it free from his collar, and the Irishman's attention swung back to him. He cursed obscenely, stepped back and dragged Henry along the floor on his knees, his fingers twisting more tightly into the cloth of Henry's collar. The blood was pounding in Henry's head and he tried to shout; his own rage was now unbridled, as humiliation and anger thrust discretion out of his mind. He had come looking for Phil Irish to get some answers, warn him of police interest, but he was being treated like a wayward puppy. He tried to rise again, roaring, but Phil Irish was strong; the powerful arm kept him down and Henry was off balance again, lurching sideways painfully on his elbow.

A chair went over with a crash, Henry's shins made painful contact with a table leg, and then he realized that Phil Irish was dragging him towards the door. It was too much; Henry surged again under the humiliation, conscious of Helen Swain crying, terrified, against the wall, but there was no effective way in which he could resist Phil Irish's power. The door was already open, where Phil had used his own key to come in, and next moment a foot was placed in Henry's back and he was propelled forcibly out to the top of the stairs. He fell forward on his face, bumping down two stairs before he was able to arrest his descent, and then he found himself in a crumpled, untidy heap staring up towards the door to Helen Swain's flat, now slammed violently in his face.

There was one long moment when Henry lay there, seemingly stupefied, his heart hammering a wild tattoo against his ribs, and then he struggled to his feet, leapt up over the stairs, hammered on the door, shouting Phil Irish's name.

When he stopped, he could hear the shouting voices inside the flat. Helen Swain was crying hysterically; Phil Irish was shouting in a flat yet violent monotone. It was as though he were detailing to Helen a long list of peccadilloes, a recreation of fault, a damning indictment of a life that had been wasted. Henry could not catch the words as such and his own mind was spinning in a curious, half-drunken way. Phil Irish was a priest taking confession; the hysterical crying of the woman was a *mea culpa* for all the sad years. Henry stopped hammering, and in a few moments the voices beyond the door ceased also. A strange, eerie silence flowed out and around Henry as he stood at the top of the stairs. He looked up and the single light bulb, unshaded, seemed to be glowing like ancient ectoplasm coming to life in the darkness. He felt dizzy, he told himself he felt sick, and he turned, wanting to go outside and drag fresh air into his lungs.

It was only a subterfuge, and he knew it. It was neither dizziness nor sickness that sent him stumbling down the stairs. It was a compound of humiliation and fear; he had been shamed by his own conduct both with Helen and with Phil Irish – he should have stayed away from her, and he should have stood up to the Irishman. He had left Helen Swain crying alone, to face the irate lover who had caught her with another man, and now he was seeking escape. But there was something else too that sent him out into the street. There was the realization that he had no real part to play in the world of those two people behind the closed door. Neither of them needed him; neither of them wanted him. Helen Swain had turned to him momentarily for a consolation that finally he could not have given her, in all probability. He was not of their world, nor did he want to be.

He stumbled out into the street. It was dark, and the street lights were showing red, glowing as they began to come to life. Henry leaned against the wall, his head down, and he became aware of someone standing in a doorway opposite, staring at him curiously, so he straightened, not wishing to draw attention to himself, and he began to walk erratically down the hill towards the main street. There must have been something unconvincing in his performance, for when he reached the corner and looked back the man had stepped out of the doorway and was still staring down the hill after Henry.

Below Henry stretched the park which led down to the backs of the houses terraced below. Henry walked through the park gates, and the courting couple sitting on the bench glared at him indignantly when he sat down beside them on the narrow seat. After a little muttering and whispering they rose and walked away, wrapped around each other, casting one last angry glance behind them.

Henry was hardly aware that they had gone.

3

It was a long night.

Henry sat on the park bench for almost two hours, thinking. There was nothing ordered about his thoughts; a confused welter of memories, distant and recent, a questioning of motive, a dreaming of pleasant events in the recent past as he indulged himself; seeking, perhaps subconsciously, to erase the unpleasantness of the last few hours and days, striving to erect a platform from which he could launch himself to a new, more sensible, structured existence. His conversation with Helen Swain had done that, at least; it had caused him to attempt to review more logically his conduct and emotions of the last few months, and if he had not yet reached a position where he could attempt to behave more positively, at least he was beginning to appreciate that basic questions needed not only to be *asked,* but to be answered. He had fallen into the trap that too many sociologists found themselves in – it was not enough merely to describe the human condition and analyse it. It was necessary, in addition, to make some attempt to remedy it, to learn from experience, to attempt a rational approach towards constructing a new condition. Hopefully, it would be better than the old, but it might even *be* the old, though viewed through different eyes.

At ten-thirty he found a fish and chip shop at the bottom of the hill, just behind the main shopping centre. They were almost ready to close, but he managed to get the last of the evening's frying, a bag of chips and a piece of cod, a pile of crisped fragments of batter. He ate them in a doorway behind the shop, and disdained environmental considerations as he dropped the newspaper into a culvert and watched it float for a while, before it became tangled with other waste against an iron grid. After that he walked for a while as the streets grew busier, noisier, and then became empty and quiet, pubs closed, cinemas out, only a few tramps for company.

At two in the morning Henry found a coffee stall and three grey-faced men on a piece of waste ground behind a bingo hall. The coffee was hot, but had little else to commend it, and the men were notably disinclined to converse. Henry leaned against the battered trunk of an old elm and watched them. It was as though he and they were the only humans left in a world of dark streets and orange-hued sky. Yet beyond the mountains lay the valley and a different world with different people, asleep in their beds, waiting for him to come back and join them, be one of them.

Henry walked.

He felt in no way tired. Phil Irish seemed to have become almost a fantasy, the death of Tommy Bighead a figment of Henry's overheated imagination. From the hill he could see the satanic skyline of the Port Talbot steelworks, a red flame in the night sky, tall brick fingers reaching, pointing upwards, a pall of industry lying over a hill and a shore and a vale. He touched his shoulders and the soreness that had never left them brought him back to a present reality, and he thought of the morning that would soon come and he sat down on a low wall, with his head against some rusty iron railings and for a little while he dozed.

His dreams were more violent than his waking thoughts. A voice boomed at him in a giant kiln and a vast white heaviness was pressing down on him, twisting out of the sky, a faint breath touching his cheek as it came. There was a body under him and one moment it was Brenda, another Helen Swain, but he himself could not move for the bar of iron that pinned him by the shoulders, riveted him to a vast, towering pillar on which a tiny, spider-figure crawled, menacing, distant, but ever-present.

He was glad for the dawn, when it came, for he was stiff and unhappy and cold. But decisive. It was over; it was finished. He had had enough.

174

There was a brief flash of early sunlight that stained the town, gave it a reddish glow, and then the clouds banked up beyond the chimneys, and the morning turned grey. Henry walked through the town on the way to the building site at Margam and he caught sight of himself in a shop window.

He looked a mess. Though his beard was not a strong one a stubble was apparent on his face, but worse than that was the generally decrepit appearance he presented. Possibly it was because he was looking at himself anew, but he looked scruffier than he had imagined of late. He guessed some of it could be put down to the fact that he had spent the night out of doors, as Jayo Davies did occasionally, that he had slept little and had no breakfast, but more than that there was the fact that he was looking at himself more critically. There had been a time when he had prided himself on his appearance – or had it been Brenda who had been insistent? He could hardly remember now.

A few workmen's buses passed him, heading for the site. He stopped at a newsagent's and managed to buy some bars of chocolate and three packets of crisps which he stuffed in his pockets. He could not even remember what had happened to his knapsack and tommybox. As he passed the railway station he discovered that the buffet was open so he got a cup of coffee and was able to get a bus from there up to the site. No one seemed interested in his appearance, and no one seemed inclined to talk. He was last off the bus, and he

175

hung back while the other workmen clocked in with Morris Weasel.

The site clerk cocked his head on one side suspiciously as Henry walked up to him. His eyes were bright and inquisitive, but they held a certain hostility also, as though he was expecting trouble from Henry, but was not resigned to it.

'What's your trouble, Jones?'

Henry hesitated. 'I'm just not certain about arrangements regarding notice,' he said. 'I mean, how much do I have to give?'

Morris Weasel's eyes widened. 'Notice? You thinkin' of packin' in, then?'

Henry nodded. 'I've decided to finish work here. I ... well...'

Morris Weasel puffed his cheeks and popped a couple of times nervously. He frowned. 'When you want to finish?'

'Well, I wouldn't want to make things awkward. End of the week, I suppose.'

'Haven't strapped at all, have you?' Morris asked, suspicion grating in his voice. 'Have to check my books, you know. Don't remember you strappin', but if you have, got to work enough shifts to cover–'

'I haven't taken any advances while I've been here,' Henry said coolly.

'No. Not from me, you haven't. But then, you're *above* that sort of thing, aren't you?' Morris sneered. 'Different from the rest, isn't it? Not really one of the boys, at all. Just playin' games, like.'

Strangely enough, though Henry would have resented the remarks a little while ago, now he

176

felt no such resentment. For in a sense, he admitted to himself, Morris Weasel was right. It had been a game. Of a sort. Morris was watching him now, expecting some reaction, but when Henry made no reply he sniffed. 'All right then. End of the week it is. At least you're givin' a bit of notice. Not like bloody Phil Irish.'

'What do you mean?' Henry asked, surprised.

'Phil Irish. First damned thing this mornin'. Only just arrived, I had, when he walked up. Never been on site that early before, he hasn't. Said he wanted payin' because he was jackin' it in.'

'He's finishing on the site?'

'That's what I just said, isn't it?' Morris Weasel popped his cheeks angrily. 'He only strapped thirty quid a few days ago, and now he walks up and says he's jackin' in the job. I tried to say he ought to work his shift today, square things and gimme time to do the books and that, but he was in a hell of a mood, I tell you, and he told me to get knotted and walked off. He's a few quid short, I think, so it's his loss. Firm's on the credit side. So if he wants to act funny...' Morris Weasel's voice died and he stared at Henry with an open curiosity. 'You look more than a bit surprised.' In the short silence that followed he took in for the first time Henry's appearance. 'What were you up to last night?'

Henry made no attempt to answer him. Instead, he asked his own question. 'Did Phil say why he was finishing work here?'

Morris Weasel's eyes narrowed. He appeared to be thinking the question over, dissecting it, examining it, looking for nuances or hidden motives behind it. Only when he failed to discover anything sinister did he speak. 'Not exactly. But I can guess.'

'Why, then?'

'Before I guess, maybe you'd like to tell me why *you* think he'd jack it in,' Morris replied evasively.

Henry hesitated. 'I've no idea,' he said at last.

'Phil said nothing to you?'

'He didn't suggest he was thinking of packing in, no.'

'Hmmm.' Morris considered for a moment, popped, then shrugged. 'Well, I don't know what's got into him, but I reckon he's thinking of going elsewhere. He's been going with that girl from The Brick Wall, they say, and maybe she's costing him too much – or maybe he's even taking her with him and moving on. I don't know which, but when I mentioned her to him this morning he was certainly a bit mad.' Morris stared at Henry curiously. 'And what you gone so red about, then?'

'Nothing. I'd better get on, or Banion will be after me.'

'Aye, that's another thing. Banion's not in yet, so he *must* be ill. That bloke, he's like a bloody machine, you know? Single-minded, if you know what I mean. Never misses a shift; always straight and so bloody sure. Bastard. No wonder no one likes him. But he's not in yet, so he won't be chasin' you. You better join the others in Twll-Mawr for this morning. But ... ah...'

Henry waited, while Morris hesitated, seemed to want to say something more. 'Yes?' he asked finally.

Morris took a deep breath. 'That gang – Phil

Irish, Jayo Davies, Tonto, Tommy ... Tommy Big-head, they ever *say* anything to you, did they?'

'About what?'

Morris seemed nonplussed, although that was exactly how Henry felt. 'Well, about...'

A man came around the corner from behind Morris Weasel's office and Morris literally jumped in nervous surprise. It was the detective-constable who had taken Henry to see the super-intendent on the first occasion they had met. His face was stiff and unsmiling. He glanced at Henry but no trace of recognition appeared in his eyes. He turned to Morris Weasel.

'Mr Morris?'

'Aye.'

'Detective-Superintendent Morgan would like a chat with you.'

'Aye, all right, I'll ... er...'

'*Now*,' the man said impassively. 'Better lock your office, though. Don't know how long you'll be, do you?'

As Morris Weasel fumbled nervously in his pocket for his keys, the detective-constable stared again at Henry. It was an uncomfortable moment for Henry; he felt as though there was something challenging in the policeman's eyes, and after a moment Henry turned away.

The sooner he left Margam and this whole unpleasant business, the better.

Henry walked across the site towards Twll-Mawr. He was uncertain to whom he should report. Jayo Davies was apparently not on site still; Phil had arrived and gone away again; that left only Tonto Thomas of the gang. Henry was not

179

particularly happy at the thought of having work assigned to him by Tonto, but perhaps there would be a foreman in Twll-Mawr who could give him a job to do.

As it happened, the situation never arose. As Henry approached Twll-Mawr he met Geordie Banion, striding around the corner from the tower block.

'You're late,' the foreman said and fixed Henry with a cold, hostile glance.

'Morris Weasel said you weren't in today,' Henry said in surprise.

'Morris don't know everything, man,' Geordie Banion snapped peevishly. Even so, Henry thought, Morris could not have been far wrong, even if Banion was on site now. Henry could guess what had happened – late arriving, Banion had not seen fit to let Morris know that his usual rigid perfection had failed him. And the reason put forward by Morris must have been right, for Banion was obviously ill, and had been suffering. His face was grey, the lines deep-marked running from the base of his nose past his mouth, and his lips were pale, twisting down discontentedly. The state of his stomach, Henry guessed, was reflected in his face. Geordie Banion looked as though he had had one hell of a gastric night and was going to make everyone pay for it this morning.

'That bloody cowboy Thomas is down in Twll-Mawr already,' Banion snarled, 'and it's time you was down there too. And what about that Irishman? You seen him?'

'He came on site this morning, but he told Mr Morris that he was finishing today. Only came for

180

his money due, I think.'

'*Finishing?*' A little devil of rage danced deep in Geordie Banion's eyes; it was as though he was taking Phil Irish's decision as an intensely personal affront. Maybe he had intended working a sweat out of the Irishman today, Henry thought, to make up for an upset stomach during the night. There had never been any love lost between the two men, that was for certain, and perhaps Banion was now regretting the fact that he would be unable to push Phil Irish hard today. 'He never said yesterday that he was packin' it in,' he muttered angrily. 'You sure he's away?'

'That's what Mr Morris said.'

Banion stood in front of Henry with his fists tightly clenched, his splay feet wide apart, and he swayed slightly. The pinched appearance of his features had become more marked and he looked far from well; the anger at hearing another of the crew had finished was obviously doing nothing for his temper. But even as Henry watched, some element of rationality returned to the foreman. His fingers loosened and he stared at Henry with eyes that hardly saw him, cold eyes with a feverish light deep within them.

'You don't look well, Mr Banion.'

'Mind your own bloody business. And get down to join Thomas – sharp!'

Henry did as he was told. It was one thing to decide he would finish at Margam at the end of the week. It was another to face up to Geordie Banion, particularly when he was in such a mood.

Crisps and chocolate were a poor substitute for

solid sandwiches of the kind Nan usually made for him, but Henry was glad enough of them during lunch break. He had to leave Twll-Mawr and tramp over to the far side of the site in order to get a cup of coffee from a stall set up there for those workmen who came without hot drinks, and when he got the coffee the cup was greasy and chipped and the coffee looked and tasted like mud. Henry's back was aching and his shoulders were sore, but at least he was glad to be out in the fresh air after the foetid stench of Twll-Mawr all morning. He had been working with strangers again; Tonto Thomas had been called out before mid-morning, and when Henry had gone to the concrete ramp where they normally assembled, he had been alone. He felt lonely in a way he had not previously felt on the site, and he was keenly aware how much he had leaned on and used the group. But now they were broken up, with Jayo Davies not having reported since Tommy Bighead died, and Phil Irish having left the site.

But it would be over by the end of the week. After that? Henry did not know. All he was certain of was that he would never return to Margam.

The afternoon was spent again in Twll-Mawr. Henry saw no sign of Tonto, or of Geordie Banion, and by four o'clock he was working virtually alone. Since there was a shortage of scaffolding tubes and clips by that time, he took the opportunity to go up above and collect a pile for the next day.

'Just as well,' the policeman in the raincoat said as Henry scrambled out of Twll-Mawr.

'What is?' Henry asked.

'I was coming down to fetch you. Save me clamberin' down there, won't it?'

'What do you want to see me for?'

The policeman smiled thinly. 'Not me, is it? I don't want to see you. It's Detective-Superintendent Morgan wants to see you. Tell you, too, I will. He's not pleased. Take it from me – he's not a bit bloody pleased, is Griff Morgan.'

CHAPTER V

1

'Not a bit pleased, I am,' Griff Morgan said as he marched up and down in the small hut that served as his office on the building site. 'Bloody angry, in fact.'

'About what?' Henry asked nervously.

'Aw, come on, boyo, you been playin' me for silly buggers, haven't you?' The heavy face was still controlled as Morgan swung around to face Henry, and the mottled cheeks were not yet empurpled as Henry guessed they would be if Morgan really worked up a rage. But there was enough hostility and unpleasantness in Morgan's eyes to suggest to Henry that he ought to play things carefully and slowly and do nothing to antagonize unnecessarily the former Cwmavon front row forward.

'I don't understand, Mr Morgan,' Henry said in a placatory tone.

'Loyalty, *I* understand,' Morgan said, and continued his short, plodding walk. 'I mean, it's instilled into you, isn't it? Poke the other bloke's eye out for your mates in the scrum; thump the lock who comes forward and clobbers your scrum-half. Aye, loyalty is something I understand, towards your mates! But these aren't *your* mates, Henry. Intelligent, you are; university educated. What you're doing here is your business of course, but you got no loyalty to these scrubbers! So what's the idea, protecting them?'

Henry's face was beginning to burn. He wet his lips. 'Protect?'

'Aye. Protecting them, that's what you been!' Morgan stopped his plunging walk and went behind the deal desk. He sat down, and became a little calmer now that he was able to deal with facts. 'Had a long chat with Morris, that little popping clerk. Tougher than he looks, you know. But he almost gave in, finally. Got a lot of it, I have, now. But I'm mad with you, Henry Jones. Not pleased at all.'

'I've not been protecting anyone!'

'Is that what you say then? I know different, see. Fact is, others have started to talk so I got a lot of the picture now. But for bits of corroboration, that's all. And you'll give me those.'

'I'll do everything I can to help,' Henry said miserably. 'But–

'No buts. Don't like buts. What I want from you is a *proper* account of the day Tommy Bighead died.'

'I told you–'

'Not enough, you didn't tell me. For instance,

184

didn't tell me what was going on, did you, that morning. Or more important, what had gone on before, isn't it!'

Henry had lost the direction of Morgan's questioning. He was adrift suddenly, not clear what the policeman wanted. He knew what he had *not* said to Morgan, and he had wanted to see Phil Irish before he supplemented his account, and that loyalty was over now, after last night. But it seemed as though Morgan wanted something more from him, and he was not clear what it could be.

'I'm sorry, I just don't—'

'All right, clever boy, let's go through it then, shall we, step by step? Let's start with the time you was down in Twll-Mawr with Jayo Davies. Got angry, didn't he? About Tommy Bighead.'

'Well, yes, he did but—'

'Threatened him, even. But you didn't tell *me* that!' Morgan's eyes were slits in his fleshy face as he glared at Henry. 'And then there was Tonto Thomas, shouting down to you in Twll-Mawr. *He* threatened to break Tommy Bighead's neck, but you didn't tell me about that, did you? Just said he was looking for Phil Irish!'

'They were just words, Mr Morgan. It was a bad morning, people were bad-tempered. It didn't mean anything—'

'Meant enough for a man to get killed! But that's not the end of the story. There was Morris Weasel, then. He came looking for the gang and he was in no good humour too, but you didn't say *that*, did you! You said damn all, Henry Jones, and I was trusting you, taking you into my confidence!'

Morgan's tone had changed. A note of insincere

sadness had entered his voice; he was injecting regret, shaking his head slightly as though he were speaking to a wayward son. There was just one second when Henry was stupefied, almost taken in by the change, and then he realized what it was all about. Morgan had said he had the picture – but he didn't. At least, not all of it. And he thought Henry could supply the missing pieces. The simulated anger had been a softening-up process, nothing more. The thought gave Henry confidence and he sat up a little straighter.

'If I did mislead you, Mr Morgan, it was inadvertent.'

'Inadvertent.' Morgan almost smacked his lips over the word. 'Good, that is. Inadvertent. But not really true, is it...? Deliberate, really. Deliberate as your general attempt to protect Phil Irish from me, by telling me so much, and not everything that went on.'

Henry moistened his lips again. 'I've not tried–'

'Oh, you have, boy, come on! But I'll play fair with you. I'll tell you what I got, and then you can see if there's point in keepin' your mouth shut any more, is it?' When Henry nodded, Morgan went on in a self-satisfied voice. 'Just good, solid police work, that's all it is, see. Ask enough questions of enough people, stick the answers all together and it's like apples in a barrel. Soon find the bad ones; if you don't, it all becomes a sticky mess you can't separate. But I found the bad ones, see. Thing is, found Jayo Davies we did – yesterday. Sleeping among the dunes, that's what he's been up to. James Olliphant Davies, open-air fiend. Too much for him, it all was on Monday, so he opted out, pulled up stakes. Quiet, he is; a mouse at heart. But, anyway, he told me about his own threats, you see, and Tonto's, and the other bits of the morning, before it all became too much and he pushed off.'

'He left before Tommy Bighead died? Left the site, I mean?'

'So he says. Worried by the quarrelling.' Morgan winked slyly. ''Course, he's bound to say that, isn't he? But we'll take it for gospel for now. Other sources of information is the foreman.'

'Mr Banion?'

'That's right. Funny chap that, in many ways. But observant. Gets up above a lot and sees things. Like the quarrel between Tommy Bighead and Phil Irish. The one *you* overheard, and didn't tell me about.'

Morgan was smiling thinly, and Henry's heart sank. The last thing he had wanted to do was to get involved in this thing; the end of the week and he could have been away. Now he was beginning to realize how foolish he had been to try to talk things out with Phil Irish before telling Morgan everything. It had only made things more difficult for himself. And when he recalled how the Irishman had humiliated him last night in front of Helen Swain, he regretted his actions even more bitterly.

'I didn't really hear anything,' Henry said shamefacedly. 'I just saw what appeared to be a quarrel.'

'But you can confirm there was an argument?'

Henry nodded. 'And Tommy Bighead called after Phil as Phil walked away. Phil sort of waved agreement reluctantly. But I don't know what it was about.'

'I do,' Morgan said, self-satisfied. 'You see, Banion's statement is pretty clear. He saw them together – he was on the flat roof across the way. He saw them arguing. And he heard what the little man shouted – though he didn't hear the rest of it. He heard, in other words, what Phil Irish and Tommy Bighead agreed to do. Know what it was?'

'No.'

'They agreed to meet in a shed, somewhere on site. We know what shed it was now, don't we, Henry?'

Henry's jaw dropped. He stared disbelievingly at the detective-superintendent. 'You're trying to say that Phil Irish knew Tommy Bighead would be in that shed, and he went up above and dropped that joist on him!'

'That's right.'

'But he wouldn't ... he'd have no reason to do it!'

'That's the point, really, Henry. Where's the motive? And that's why you're here right now. Because you didn't tell me everything, did you?'

'I've told you all I know now and–'

'Have you, hell! I could knock it out of you, young Jones, like I used to knock it out of some pussyfootin' half backs in the old days. But I'll give you a chance. I'll make it easy. I'll give you facts, and you can come up with your own theories! All right?'

Henry nodded nervously. Morgan began.

'Had a long talk with Jayo Davies, now, and today with Morris Weasel. Jayo is open enough, but don't know enough. Tonto Thomas still got his mouth shut. Morris Weasel is scared. He's come half-way clean, but isn't finished squealing yet. But the basic facts are these: like I said earlier, there's a fiddle being worked on this site. Not big, but big enough. Simple too. Morris Weasel is the collector. He knows what comes on the site and keeps books. He also keeps a funny little black book in his waistcoat. Got rid of it he has, somewhere, but we'll find it. And my guess is it'll give us a record of just what was being stolen from the site, by way of materials.'

'And you're suggesting Phil–'

'I *know* that your gang was involved. Not you personally, because you were *different*, and they didn't know how you'd jump. But Phil Irish, Tonto Thomas and Jayo Davies were all tied in with Morris. The first two did most of the lifting; Jayo's job was merely to keep an eye on things during the day.'

The endless perambulations, the creeping into bunkers, boxes in dark corners. It *had* formed part of a pattern of activity, after all. Jayo, ostensibly lazing and hiding away, in reality also making sure materials were undisturbed. 'But if I'd been more experienced, less blind, I'd have latched on,' Henry said. 'I mean, I was with Jayo–'

'They had no choice about that. When Banion assigned you to Jayo it was awkward, but, like you said, you were too blind to see what was going on. And going around looking for clips and tubes, it was easy for Jayo to keep an eye on things. Unsuspected. Then, night times, Young Beckie the night-watchman was too deaf to be aware that the lorry was coming on site, late, to pick up the materials.'

'But where did Tommy Bighead fit into this?'

'Well, I'll tell you ... Tommy Bighead had been around a bit. His character made him move, but the spinoff was that he had contacts on most of the sites. You see, this isn't just an isolated thing. All right, Phil Irish and Jayo Davies and Morris are small time enough, but what if the same thing is happening all over? And I think it is. That means there'll be a Tommy Bighead on every site you can name.'

'I don't understand.'

'Link-man. Tommy Bighead was a go-between. And there'll be more than a few like him, I reckon.'

'But linking with whom?'

Morgan smiled blandly. 'With the man – or group of men – who are organizing these petty thefts from individual sites. For remember, a lot of petty thefts mean, in the end, a pretty large thieving operation. Maybe throughout West Wales.'

Henry was silent. It was beginning to make sense to him now. The group he had joined had never been one which had close ties. He had looked at it and seen it as a society of misfits. They had nothing in common with each other; he had thought they had been bound together by a social need. In fact, they had never needed each other, except in one basic way. Petty criminal activity. And though Tonto Thomas and Jayo and Phil had disliked, even *hated* the little man with the encephalitic head, they accepted him because he was a link-man with the organizers, the men who paid.

'I remember Tommy Bighead telling Phil Irish it paid Phil to keep Tonto Thomas's temper in check. He sneered, said he was *good* to Phil.'

'And so he was. Link-man and payer-out. That's why Tommy Bighead died with a hundred and fifty quid on him. It was payout money. That never got paid.'

'But why was Tommy killed?'

'I hoped you could tell me that,' Morgan said slowly. 'By telling me what was going on that morning. And what had happened before.'

'But there's nothing I can add. It was just an atmosphere and before that–'

'Look, son, there was an atmosphere all right. Banion recognized it, Jayo admitted it, Morris accepts it, though Tonto Thomas says nothing. But they were all at each other's throats that morning. *Why?* What had happened before? Or that morning?'

'That morning ... nothing.' Henry thought hard, and then a light began to glimmer in his mind. There was something else too, a link that he almost saw before it drifted away again. 'The only thing that happened,' he said slowly, 'was the fight in the night-club.'

'The Brick Wall?'

'That's right. Friday night. Phil Irish got a bit drunk, tangled with Tonto Thomas, and got thrown out. That's why Tonto was snarling at Phil that morning–'

'But what did Tommy Bighead have to do with that?' Morgan frowned thoughtfully. 'Why would it cause so much unpleasantness on site? An argument between two–'

'Ah, there was something else about it, too,' Henry interrupted. 'There's something else I should remember, something about...' His voice faded away. He shook his head as though trying to clear it. A voice in a tunnel, a woman's voice, and yet it wasn't a woman's voice at all. Someone else, disjointed, a vowel sound...

'The kilns,' he said, and Morgan looked at him in surprise. 'I told you about the kilns.'

'No,' Morgan said harshly, 'you didn't.'

Henry told him, without apology. His voice became more excited, his speech faster as the significance of it all dawned on him. 'I followed Phil Irish to those kilns, and I think now, with hindsight, that it would have been Morris Weasel in there with him. But Mr Banion will probably be able to confirm that. He watched, after I'd gone. But the important thing is what was said in the kilns – and what I heard. My name ... and something else. *Ardour.*'

'What the hell has sex got to do with this?' Morgan snapped impatiently.

'You miss the point, as I did. The words were broken, disjointed. That's how the sound came to me and it meant nothing. But last night, after you dropped me, I met a girl. And at one point she spoke of her employer. Arfon Rhayader. And something about it struck a chord in my mind.'

'I don't follow.'

'*I* pronounce the name with the accent on the first syllable. *Rhay*ader. She didn't. Like a number of people in the Margam area she uses a different inflexion. *She placed emphasis on the second syllable.*'

Gryfydd Morgan looked at him blankly for a moment and then tried it gingerly. 'Rha*yard*er,' he said. 'Aye, people down at West Dock say it that way. Like that name *Main*waring. Some clowns call it "Mannering". But so what?'

'Now ask Morris Weasel to say the name,' Henry said triumphantly.

Morgan was silent. He turned in his chair, stared out of the window for several minutes, before swinging back to Henry. 'Said you was clever, didn't I? University educated. So go on. Tell me the rest of it.'

Henry came out with it in a rush. It was as though floodgates had been released in his mind and theories tumbled out, interlocking pieces fitted, almost the whole puzzle took shape. 'Tommy Bighead was a link-man who paid the site gang for what they stole. But there had to be an organizer, someone who met the people who bought and sold the stolen building materials. Where better could this be done than in a night-club? Arfon Rhayader's night-club!'

'Go on.'

'There's a girl there. Helen Swain. She told me last night that while she's been working there she's seen Rhayader working on the fringes of criminal activity, small stuff–'

'That's known, right enough,' Morgan admitted.

'Well, I think he's right at the centre of this web too,' Henry urged. 'You see, I know why things went skyhigh on Monday morning. On Friday night there was a fight in the night-club. Arfon Rhayader threw Phil Irish out. He was as mad as hell at Phil knocking things about in the club. Now

what I think happened is this: Tommy Bighead
made contact with Rhayader over the weekend
and got told that Phil Irish had to be dropped.
Either that, or he warned Tommy Bighead that
Phil had to be kept out of the club in future or
Rhayader would cut them all off. *That's* why they
were all so upset and angry with Phil Irish on
Monday morning. I saw Morris and Tonto and
Tommy all wanting to cross swords with Phil because he had endangered – maybe was endanger-
ing further – their system for thefts on the site.'

'And the kilns?'

'That came after. I think Morris was scared I
might be starting to suspect the truth and he
wanted to have a talk with Phil. My name was
certainly mentioned, and Phil probably told him
the truth of the matter – that though I worked with
the gang on the site I didn't know anything. I
hadn't been brought into their schemes, and I
hadn't been bright enough to cotton on to what
was happening. But one or the other of them
mentioned Rhayader's name. My guess is it would
have been Morris – maybe he was still concerned
about the system being broken open, maybe he
was criticizing Phil for upsetting everything on
account of his wild temper. Maybe–'

'Lot of maybes,' Morgan interrupted. He eyed
Henry carefully. 'Lot of graduates come in the
police these days, you know. Accelerated
promotion, they get. But I played with bright lads
before – Cwmavon, now, had nine teachers and six
colliers in the side after I packed in. Had flair, they
did, the bright boys, bit of imagination, like. In the
backs, of course. So I got no down on graduates –

194

they can do the thinking for you sometimes. And you been doing a bit of thinking, Henry. A lot of maybes, yes, but you been thinking...' He smiled coldly and cautiously. 'But, aye, it fits, you know. Arfon Rhayader, we've had our eye on him for a while now, but one of the troubles has always been he knows too many bigwigs, councillors and that sort of thing, so before you move against a man like Rhayader you got to have the goods on him. We been building a dossier but things are difficult to prove. Theft, a bit of corruption ... people don't take it too seriously. But murder, now, that's a different thing. If we could show Arfon Rhayader was tied up, even at the edges, with Tommy Bighead's death, we could maybe clobber him well and good. Aye, Rhayader could be the ringleader all right, and if he was niggled over that fight in his night-club he could have put pressure on the site gang, through Tommy Bighead. And they'd have turned on Phil Irish, sure enough. It fits, boyo, it makes sense.'

Henry hesitated. 'It still doesn't amount to any proof that it was Phil Irish who killed Tommy. The motive–'

'We got evidence that says Phil Irish knew Tommy Bighead would be in that shed at a certain time. Arranged to meet him there, he had. Now what if Phil Irish was fed up with all the niggling? What if he was sick of being needled? What if Tommy Bighead was set on paying him off – or not paying him his due? Any of these reasons could be enough to send a wild man like that Irish yob up above to heave a concrete joist on the little man.'

'But he had a hundred and fifty pounds on him,' Henry argued.

'Okay, but we don't know Phil Irish knew that. Anyway, no matter. He had a short temper – the night-club incident told us that. Anything could have sparked him. It's enough for me that he was having a quarrel with Tommy Bighead, and that the little man got killed in a place where they'd agreed to meet.'

'It's true that Phil can go berserk when he's drunk, but–'

The phone on Morgan's deal desk rang stridently and insistently. Morgan lifted the receiver, cradled it into his neck while he lit a cigarette and listened. Henry waited. There was a fine tracery of red veins in the policeman's nose and Henry followed the tiny broken lines as though seeking his way out of a maze. There was an occasional grunt from Morgan, but nothing was to be read in his face. Twice his glance flickered up to Henry, and then away again. Once, testily, he exclaimed, 'But where's the connection with *this?*' and then settled down to listen again. At last he grunted again, contemplated the wall as both he and receiver stayed silent, and then he said, 'All right. We'll be down.'

He replaced the receiver, glared distastefully at his cigarette. 'Kept off these when I was playing. Had other weaknesses then, like girls. You got a weakness like that, Henry?'

Henry shook his head and Morgan smiled. 'Don't believe it, good-looking lad like you. Besides, you was with a girl last night. Told me, you did.'

'Yes. Helen Swain.'

'Took her home, didn't you? Oh, don't trouble to deny it. Left your knapsack in her flat, see. That's what the call was about.'

'My knapsack?' Henry asked, puzzled.

'Not exactly...What was it I said, Henry? About Phil Irish having a short temper. You the same, are you?'

'I don't understand.'

''Course you do, *bach*. Intelligent lad like you! Damn, I know the feeling, like. Tell you, there was a time when we used to make a tour of the South West every Easter. Bloody good time we had, three games, tight every night, introduce a couple of horses into the lounge of the hotel for a laugh, tap on an old lady's bedroom window middle of the night for a giggle, you know, all that sort of nonsense. But one year we been to a dance, one of the back row, he picked up a bird and ended up in the sack with her. Well, once is enough, see, so next night he didn't want to know, but she came pestering around in the hotel. He didn't want her, so I took her off his neck, so to speak. Going great we were, at midnight, in my room, when suddenly she sort of realized she wasn't with the same bloke as the night before and she changed her mind. So I know the feeling.'

Henry stared at Morgan, not understanding what the policeman was talking about. 'What feeling?'

Morgan scratched his nose thoughtfully. 'Making it hard, you are, Henry. Look, I'll tell you. Investigation of Tommy Bighead's death, we make all sort of inquiries, and we take a look at all the people who knew him. Now then, one chap we look at is Phil Irish, natural. And we hear he's got a girl-friend. Now then, last night I dropped you off at The Brick Wall, and next thing you tell me you took this girl home. Helen Swain. Phil Irish's girl. And down at Port Talbot station there's a phone call this afternoon. Neighbours. Reckon they heard some shouting last night, and again this morning. Woman screaming. Don't like to interfere, but didn't see her come out as usual today, so in the end they take a look upstairs, nosey like. And then they call the police.'

'But what's happened?'

'We'll go down and see, Henry *bach*, we'll go down and see. And then you can tell me what it was Helen Swain said after you laid her last night – what it was that so upset you that you almost beat her to death!'

2

'Now then, Mr Jones, what have you got to say about this, then?'

Detective-Superintendent Morgan stepped aside slightly to allow Henry to enter the flat. It was a shambles. Both easy chairs had been overturned, the table leg was broken and several cups lay shattered on the floor. There was a smear of blood on the wall near the window as though someone had tried to wipe his hands, and with a table lamp overturned, books thrown about and almost every article in the room hurled down, it was as though a tornado had swept through the room.

'Angry, was you?' Morgan asked coldly.

'But I didn't do this,' Henry said thickly.

'That your knapsack over there?'

'Yes, but–'

'And you did come here with her last night, after I dropped you near The Brick Wall?'

'Well, of course I did,' Henry admitted, 'but I didn't stay that long. I left about nine, or thereabouts.'

Gryfydd Morgan looked at him owlishly and pursed his lips. 'Why is that, then?' he asked.

Henry made no reply. He was not certain what held back the words. It was easy enough to tell Morgan he had left, humiliated, after Phil Irish had burst in on him and Helen Swain, and yet the words stuck in his throat. Perhaps it was partly because he did not want to tell the full story, or perhaps it was because he still could not understand how – or believe that – Phil Irish would have gone berserk in this way. And yet.

'Well?' Morgan waited for a moment and then turned to the detective-constable standing just inside the door behind them. 'Evans, you've seen the woman. What's the extent of her injuries?'

'Can only give a superficial estimate at this stage, sir,' the constable said seriously. 'I mean, the medics at the hospital haven't done a complete check yet. But up to now we know she's got a fractured skull, abrasions on the forehead and about the eyes, considerable cutting on the cheeks–'

'Cutting?'

'Not deep, sir, probably the result of the assailant wearing gloves, surface ripping the skin, that sort of thing, sir. Cracked cheekbone, they think; severe bruising of the breasts and stomach and along the inside of the left thigh–'

'Sexual attack?'

The detective-constable shrugged. 'Bit early to say, sir. Clothes were torn a bit, as you might imagine, but the bruising on the whole seems to be the result of *punching*.' He wrinkled his nose suddenly, in distaste. 'It's possible she was hammered to make her submit to rape, but it doesn't look as though she *was* raped. So if the motive was sexual, it's probable the act wasn't completed. Maybe he was disturbed, ran away...'

His voice died as the detective-superintendent stared stonily at him. 'Theories come later, Evans,' Morgan said coldly. 'Facts, first. And the facts we got so far are that she was knocked about a bit, and the flat was pulled apart, and,' he added, turning again to Henry, '*you* were here.'

'And left at nine,' Henry insisted.

Morgan grunted. He turned away from Henry, walked into the bedroom. Henry followed. The bed was unmade, but there was little sign of violence in the room, apart from the fact that most of Helen Swain's clothes had been dragged out of the wardrobe, some of them ripped, her personal possessions scattered about the room, the drawers of the chest against the wall tipped out on to the floor. Henry moistened his lips.

'Burglary?' he suggested.

Morgan looked at him scornfully. '*You* wear gloves, Henry?'

'I tell you I left at nine! And she was all right when I left. At least–'

'Yes?'

Henry hesitated. The images that came into his mind were confused. He thought back to The Brick Wall, and the way that Phil Irish had been fighting mad, hurling himself at Tonto Thomas and his brother. He thought of the alley and the prone figure huddled in the darkness after Rhayader's thugs had showed their expertise. But it was all mixed up with another image – Phil Irish, shouting, almost beside himself last night as he caught Helen in Henry's arms.

'You got to admit, Henry,' Morgan said softly, 'things look bad for you. I mean, you go to the club, pick her up, bring her back here – and there, next morning, she's all beat up. It happened, apparently, early this morning, but no doubt you can account for your whereabouts ... if you wasn't here.'

'I ... I just walked about all night,' Henry said miserably.

'Just ... walked ... about.'

'Slept in the park.'

A pleading, insincere note entered Morgan's voice. 'You see how it is, Henry? Things do look bad, don't they? Unless you got something else to say. Like you know who *really* done it.'

'I...' There was a tight, panicked feeling in Henry's chest. He knew exactly what Brenda would have advised him to do in this situation. He could not explain to himself why he held back. And yet, was he right to refuse to reply? After all, he had wanted to protect Phil Irish from suspicion over Tommy Bighead's death and where had that got him? Near to a beating last night.

201

It was possible that the beating had been given to Helen. And Henry thought of the silence that had fallen in the room, while he had stood outside in his humiliation.

'Phil Irish,' he said, and the words were gone beyond recall.

Morgan pounced on the name like a cat on a mouse. 'He was here last night?'

'He ... he came in ... and suggested I leave.'

'*Suggested?*'

Henry was unable to meet the detective-superintendent's eye. 'He threw me out,' he said unhappily.

'So he was mad, catching you with Helen Swain – his girl-friend?' When Henry made no reply, Morgan grinned, satisfied. 'It'll do, boy, it'll do. Didn't really think it could have been you. Too soft, you are, to do something wild like this. Needs a man with *passion*, it does. Not enough good red blood in your veins to get you worked up hard. You see, Henry, when a man lays into a woman the way Helen Swain's been hammered, it means that he *cares.* Oh, all right, it may be he's caring more about himself than he is about her, you know, he's self-centred, feels betrayed, his manhood called into question, that sort of thing. Or maybe it's just frustration – you know, all pent-up for a long time and it bursts out like a ragin' flood, and sweeps everything away – common sense, control, values. But it's got to be based on *care,* hasn't it? Helen Swain's got to be important to the man who knocked her about that way. And you don't care that much about her. She wasn't important to you. Just a bit of fun, that's all.' He glanced quizzically at Henry. 'See what I mean? But she could be important to Phil Irish. His girl-friend. Heading for the sack with another feller. And a mate at that. Enough to drive a man over the edge, if he's got a violent streak already. And your mucker Phil's got a violent streak all right. Hasn't he?'

'Yes.'

'There you are, then.'

Henry put out a hand. 'Frustration,' he said.

'What?'

'You mentioned frustration.'

'So?'

'When Phil came back last night and caught me here he ... he was mad all right. Started shouting at her, yelling, maybe shaking her about and that sort of thing. And he's violent all right. But there's someone else who's violent – and who's frus-trated, too.'

'Violence and frustration aren't enough in them-selves,' Morgan said reflectively, scratching his nose. 'But you got somebody in mind, connected with Helen Swain–'

'And with Phil Irish,' Henry suggested. 'And if you're right in all the guessing, with the fiddles on the site, too.'

'Tell me.'

'Arfon Rhayader.'

Morgan hesitated, turned, walked out of the bedroom and picked up one of the easy chairs, righted it, and sat down in it. He looked up at Henry and smiled a pleased smile. 'You know,' he said, shaking his head in mock admiration, 'I like a bloke with a one-track mind. I bet that if I came to you with just about any crime arisin' in West Wales you'd find some way of laying it at Arfon Rhayader's door. Not that I *mind*, of course!' he added, raising a hand as though to ward off Henry's unspoken protests. 'But you got to have proof before you make such statements, *bach*.'

'Well of course I don't have proof. But neither have you against me or against Phil Irish.'

'Only a moment ago–'

'I know, I said Phil Irish could have done it. But that's not the only circumstantial evidence around.'

'So tell me,' Morgan said quietly.

'At the club that night, when there was the fight, Rhayader came across to the table, and Helen told me about him. He's been after her for months. It's one of the reasons he was so vicious about Phil Irish. It was part frustration, not just Phil wrecking his night-club.'

'And you think it could be Arfon Rhayader who hammered Helen last night?'

'I don't know! But I don't think you should jump to conclusions about Phil. All right, *I* was here – but I left before it happened. And *Phil* was here – why couldn't he have left before it happened?'

'But why should Rhayader *want* to knock her about last night?' Morgan asked. 'Why should he come around after you and the Irishman had gone, and lay into her?'

'He sacked her,' Henry said quickly. 'He sacked her a week ago. Then he regretted it. She told me–'

'Why did he sack her?'

Henry shook his head impatiently. 'He was mad about the fight. Mad about the fact she wouldn't sleep with him. He said he'd had a lot of bad luck since she came there – vandalism, broken lights, that sort of thing. But she told me he changed his mind about sacking her. He asked her to stay on.'

'So?'

'Well, don't you see? Phil was here last night. He was mad with her. But they *could* have made things up. Morris Weasel told me this morning that Phil got mad when he guessed maybe Phil was packing in at Margam to go off with Helen Swain. Now what if that was the idea? What if Phil and Helen had decided to leave Margam, go elsewhere?'

'I don't see no motive there for Rhayader to bash her,' Morgan growled impatiently.

'I got the impression Rhayader doesn't forgive easily,' Henry insisted. 'Helen hinted to me that she knew enough scraps of information to cause Rhayader trouble; he was already frustrated by her refusals; he was angry with Phil Irish for the fight at the club; things were going awry at the North Margam site with Tommy Bighead's death and you questioning Morris and the rest of us; and now Helen insists she's leaving, and is going off with Phil Irish! Why isn't it possible that Rhayader went around there last night, maybe to put some pressure on her, maybe to have one last crack at sleeping with her?'

Morgan showed his teeth in a wide, doubtful grimace. He shook his head slowly. 'Thin, it is. But ... well, let's just give it a try, hey? *Evans!*'

The detective-constable appeared in the door

like a startled rabbit. 'Sir?'

'Get the car.'

Morgan made no attempt at conversation during the drive down town to The Brick Wall. He told Henry to stay in the car while he went into the night-club with Evans. Henry sat staring at the back of the driver's neck. It was reddish, and the skin was marked with old boil scars. The driver did not speak to Henry but stared straight ahead, and his constant finger-drumming on the dashboard irritated Henry, mainly because he could not recognize the rhythm.

Within twenty minutes Morgan emerged, climbed into the car, and once Evans had taken the front seat, ordered the driver to return to the North Margam site. Not until they turned in past Young Beckie's hut did Henry have sufficient courage to ask Morgan what he had learned at The Brick Wall.

'Learned?' Morgan asked. 'Nothing. Fact is, Arfon Rhayader hasn't been near the club in twenty-four hours. Unusual, that is. But not in-explicable for a man with his business dealings, straight and nefarious. So, we're no further forward. But I'll say this, Henry Jones. Maybe you got a fixation about Arfon Rhayader. Maybe you're just tryin' to protect your mucker Phil Irish – though God knows why you want to protect a dumb Irishman who's put the screws on you! Even so, I'd be more than pleased if we *could* tie in that bastard. But I wouldn't put money on it. My cash would go straight on that bloody Irishman. In my book, he dropped that joist on Tommy Bighead, and he also hammered that girl. When – or if – she regains consciousness she'll tell us something, at least. But I never did like waiting. So right now there's a call out for your precious Irishman. And me, I'm going to put the fears of hell into that crooked site clerk Morris Weasel. Then Tonto Thomas. And then you again, young Jones. So don't go away. I'll be wanting to see you again before the day's out. So stay on site until I call you.'

The last Henry saw of him he was striding away towards Morris Weasel's hut as though he was going to take it apart plank by plank.

3

The hypothesis Henry had expounded to Gryfydd Morgan was not an impossible or even improbable one. It had been built upon facts and founded in events which Henry had personally witnessed. To a certain extent he had succeeded in raising doubts in Morgan's mind; to a certain extent Henry even believed in the theory himself. It was possible that Arfon Rhayader had beaten Helen Swain viciously in a mixture of anger at Phil Irish's interference in his affairs and frustration at Helen's refusals. But there was something tenuous about it all; it had come glibly to Henry's tongue because he had been nettled at Morgan's easy assumption that either Henry or Phil Irish had committed the assault.

Henry thought about it further while he was clearing the roof area to which Geordie Banion had sent him on his return. The foreman still looked ill, but had recovered to a certain extent, in that he was less grey and the lines around his mouth were less marked. If his health was improving his temper was not, however, and he railed on at Henry for several minutes about the shortage of labour that afternoon and what did the police think they were bloody well playing at? They'd taken Henry off joyriding, Tonto Thomas had been questioned again, Phil Irish had left the site, Jayo Davies, it seemed, had no intention of returning, and what the hell could Banion do with a series of temporary scaffolders and one inexperienced mate?

But it was quieter on the roof after Banion had stalked off among the girders above, nettled at Henry's disinclination to talk about what he had been doing with Morgan. The fact was, Henry did not want to talk about it because he was in as confused a state as he had ever been at Margam. Only this morning he had decided to break free from the insubstantial ties that held him to the site, and return to the Rhondda, never to set foot in Margam again. And yet there he had been this afternoon, defending Phil Irish, and digging even more deeply into matters that did not and should not concern him. This was *not* his world. He had discarded it, and the sooner he was away, the better.

More than that was the fear that lay quiescent in Henry's stomach; quiescent, but ready to leap into terrified life. For up there on the roof, with a darkening sky about him and the wind picking up in strength, moaning around the walls, tearing at plastic sheeting and pulling at him as he dis-

208

mantled the scaffolding, he was able to look down and see the height from which a concrete joist had fallen, the tiny size of men and materials from this distance, and experience to a certain degree the feelings of the man who had dropped that piece of concrete over the edge.

And he knew in his heart that Phil Irish could have done it. The man was slow, and not moved swiftly to anger, but Henry had seen him in many of his moods, and the scene at The Brick Wall was firmly planted in his mind, as was the occasion when Henry himself had been the recipient of Phil's violence – curbed, it was true, but Henry recalled the way those knuckles had dug into his neck, and he knew that if Phil Irish had got angry enough he could have killed Tommy Bighead. And beaten Helen Swain.

But if Phil Irish had beaten the girl so badly and if he could nurse the sort of grudge that had caused him to kill Tommy Bighead as deliberately as squashing a fly, there was the likelihood that he had not finished paying off his scores. Henry had no illusions about the matter. Phil Irish was in a dangerous state. His temper had broken up a system of thieving on the site and had cost him money and his job; a man had died as a result of that temper, and a woman had been badly beaten. It followed from this, in Henry's judgement, that Henry Jones could be the next in line. After all, it was he who had been making love to Phil Irish's girl last night. Phil's anger had been directed initially towards Helen and he had merely thrown Henry out of the flat. But during the night his brooding had turned to violence, he had beaten the girl in a savage thrust of anger in the early hours of the morning, and then he had turned up at Margam to claim his money.

Ostensibly.

But Morris Weasel had said he had little coming, if any. So perhaps he had used the money as an excuse. There could have been another reason for appearing on site.

He wanted to get even with Henry Jones.

The fear in Henry's stomach lifted sourly, fluttered against his ribs. Reason told him that Phil Irish could have hammered him when he had the chance, last night in the flat. But men did not behave reasonably; when they were overtaken by anger or desire or obsession they could behave irrationally, conduct themselves like madmen, and Phil Irish could have built up his anger, stoked it through the night hours until in the cold dawn he had beaten Helen and now wanted to take the chance he had missed last night – and attack Henry Jones.

The people far below looked tiny and insignificant. Phil had killed Tommy Bighead with the kind of deliberate cool commitment that denoted a single-mindedness, dangerous in itself. If he had come to the site this morning, looking for Henry, he would hardly have turned away and forgotten about it when he missed him in the first instance.

It became so clear now to Henry. Phil would have thought Henry had gone home. He would have waited for the morning train from the Rhondda. When Henry was not on it he would have come up to the site with the Rhondda men.

It was only by good fortune that Henry had missed him. *But where had Phil Irish gone then?*

The iron clip clanged noisily on the concrete roof as it fell from Henry's numb fingers. He walked across to the edge of the roof, placed his hands on the guard rail, tapped his boot against the toe board as though assuring himself it was really there, and then he looked over the edge and down.

The North Margam building site spread out beneath him. The holes in the ground were like the boil scars on the back of the police driver's neck. There were deep shadows and encrustations, brick walls and chimneys, decayed, broken, and new structures. It was an unholy, discordant jungle, grey and black and brown, an amalgam of stone and brick and destruction. There was something soulless about its lack of planning, something unreal and something inhuman. It was as though it existed independently of man; it was not his creation and it would never be his servant. Henry stared at the site and felt that in some inexplicable way it had had a life of its own and always would. Workmen might move in with their explosives and their bricks, their scaffolding and their steel, but North Margam would never change essentially. It had resisted governments and individuals; it had never succumbed to the formalization of an industrial complex; it was itself, a bleak landscape of torn earth that bore the signs of man's ravaging but had never surrendered to his will.

And in a strange, frightening way, Henry thought that it was essentially *responsible* for the death of Tommy Bighead, responsible for the

211

death, and the hiding of his murderer.

Henry could see Gryfydd Morgan's car parked near Morris Weasel's office. There was a certain amount of activity there; men standing outside, a policeman walking away across the site, Gryfydd Morgan himself standing in the doorway, hands on his broad hips, a front row forward awaiting the next phase of play. Elsewhere, across the site, Henry could see the usual drifting of activity away from the periphery towards the centre of the site, the gates, the ending of the day drift. But the site itself seemed to lie there with a malignant satisfaction, a great broken-backed beast, suffering from its wounds but nursing somewhere in its heart a man who had killed and whom, at the appropriate time, it would release again. Henry shook his head, attempting to remove the fanciful, dangerous thoughts that were crowding in on him. Anthropomorphic concepts were for primitives, not for an educated, modern man who had learned all about social complexes and guilts and fears and *mores*. And yet they were there in his brain, and the site was his enemy.

Until he *felt* the faint vibration in the guard rail.

The flat concrete roof was perhaps eighty feet above ground level. It was both Phil Irish and Tonto Thomas who had told Henry he should not work above ninety feet without extra pay. The warning now seemed to have been given an age ago, so much seemed to have happened in the meantime. On this occasion Geordie Banion had certainly given Henry a job below the relevant height but it was still high, and access to the first two floors of the structure was by boarded-back concrete stairs. Above that, it was necessary to climb the scaffolding. And the vibration in the guard rail had been caused by something – a steel-capped boot, perhaps – clanging against the scaffolding below.

Henry looked down to the sheer sides of the building. The scaffolding was an intricate web of steel and aluminium tubing, crossing and criss-crossing in angular fashion, a whole series of squares and diagonals and triangles that never failed to fascinate Henry in their intricacy. At intervals there were boardwalks, positioned to make it easier for workmen to climb above or to provide platforms for brickies and plasterers and painters and welders. But the scaffolding ran high, right up to the level of the roof on which Henry stood, and its top rail served as the guard that ran right around the roof area.

Henry could see no one on the scaffolding below. He looked up and about him. The sky was heavy and grey, a hint of rain in the wind. Across the flat roof, in the shadow of the broad chimney that would eventually serve as air vent and heat circulator, was a pile of bricks, and beyond that the scaffolding rose again, tied into the concrete breeze blocks, making a climbing frame that rose thirty feet above Henry's head and linked to the catwalk that ran across to the next building, twenty feet distant.

Henry was alone on the roof.

Even as the thought crossed his mind he heard the whistle shriek. It was the end of the shift. The men had been making their way down and across the site for the last ten minutes. Only Henry remained up above, and there was someone on the scaffolding below him.

He released the guard rail. He ran across to the other side of the roof, leaned against the rail and looked down again. No one. But again there came the faint, clanging tremor in the rail, and the sourness inside Henry twisted and rose as he ran to the third side and the fourth, peering over, leaning out to try to see down into the maze of scaffolding and boardwork. Someone was down there, climbing; Henry knew it, but he could see no one. The boards obscured his view, but he did not need to see, really. He knew who it would be. The site had hidden him all through the day; Jayo Davies's bunkers and dark places had concealed him; but the day was over and Henry was on the roof and it was time to come and settle outstanding scores.

Henry's mouth was dry and his hand was shaking slightly. He knew he was no match for the powerful Irishman, particularly when committed to a course he had brooded on all day in the darkness of some evil-smelling pit. The only thing Henry could think of, momentarily, was escape. If he could swing out on to the clear side of the scaffolding he could climb down quietly, make his way to the ground. But even as he thought of it, and felt the tremor in the guard rail again, his heart sank. He knew he'd never make it. He was notoriously slow in his descent; he was unnerved by the height; any workman on the site could move twice as fast as he; and perhaps most importantly, on the scaffolding itself he would be helpless, a prey to be picked off by a strong, confident hand.

There was only one thing for it. Henry had to face the danger. And even up the odds.

He knew he was no match for the maddened Irishman. But there was one thing he could do. He stood irresolute for a moment, looking about him, glaring at the pile of bricks, the various tools left on the roof, the clump of iron clips that Henry had piled in one corner. But at last he walked across to the heap of scaffolding tubes he had collected during the latter part of the afternoon.

They lay there in a rusting pile, heavy, inert, iron, aluminium. The scaffolding that Henry had demolished had stood against the chimney stack, and of necessity it had demanded above-average lengths. Normally, most of the tubes were eight feet long or more; nine-footers were common, and some of the uprights were between twelve and fifteen feet long. They were the ones which lacerated Henry's shoulder muscles until Granda had sewn in the shoulder pads. But there were six-foot lengths too, and it was one of these that Henry now looked for. Six feet of tubing; it was all he wanted, and for an agonized thirty seconds he thought there would not be one there in the pile. Then he saw one, grabbed at the end of it, tugged, and the whole pile twisted, surged, fell sideways and rolled, clattering and clanking across the concrete roof.

Henry picked up the six-foot pole and ran. He turned behind the square edge of the chimney stack and stood there, trembling, with the scaffolding tube clenched in his right hand, to attention beside him. He felt sick, but determined, and though a nervous excitement made his whole body shake there was something else building up inside him too, an ancient, atavistic desire for violent activity that would tear him from his civilized state until he could be as much of a beast as the man who had murdered Tommy Bighead and battered Helen Swain.

Next moment he heard the clatter of a steel-capped working boot as the man climbed over the guard rail on the other side of the roof and stepped down on to the concrete.

There were many things that ran through Henry's mind in the following seconds. To a certain extent a calmness descended upon him, and he was able to contemplate with a surprising equanimity the situation in which he found himself. In a curious way he seemed to find an inevitability in it all: the progression to this concrete roof and a confrontation with a near-madman seemed the logical finale to the first mistaken decision Henry had made – the decision to come to North Margam at all. That decision had been compounded by others – an attachment to a gang that had been obviously ill-suited and bound together only by a common self-interest; an involvement with a woman who had an unhappy, doubtful past and a man who was inclined towards criminal violence; a refusal to accept the demands of his home and his background and the responsibilities placed upon him by his friends; and an insistence that Phil Irish could not have been so coldly vicious as to crash down a concrete joist and smash a fist into a woman's face. The inevitability of it all now found an echo in the commitment that arose in Henry's veins. He knew what he had to do, and what he was going to do. There was now no question of finding excuses for Phil Irish; there was to be no hesitation, no asking for answers to problems that puzzled him. Henry had to act before his enemy acted. It was a time for decision.

What was it that Helen Swain had said to him last night? The words still lingered on in his mind.

'You got to commit yourself in the end. Got to *decide*, you have. Decisions can raise more problems than you're facing, and it takes courage to take a decision, but you can't just go on hoping. Got to act, you have. And when you commit yourself, follow it through.'

The steps rang out on the concrete roof and Henry took his decision, committed himself, and with the six-foot scaffolding tube in his hands leapt out from cover to face the man who had been his friend.

It could have been no more than two seconds, and yet it seemed an hour to Henry. Phil Irish had been striding out across the flat roof and Henry's emergence from behind the chimney stack stopped him dead in his tracks. His rugged features registered surprise, a slow-witted man confronted by something unexpected, and he stood rooted to the spot, unable to think, unable to speak. In that long two seconds as they stared at each other Henry saw how Phil Irish's face seemed to have changed. There was a greyish tinge under his skin and he looked as though he had slept badly. There was a rumpled look about his mouth and he was grimacing, drawing the lines close together around his eyes as though seeking to shield them from a pain he had not been forewarned of. His mouth was open, slack; and though his fists were clenched his arms hung loosely, almost hopelessly, as though something had gone from his life. They stared at each other, and the first reactions changed Phil Irish's face, the eyes came alive, and in that moment Henry shouted and swung the scaffolding tube.

If he had swung for Phil Irish's head he would surely have killed him. Henry had not decided upon a course of action; he had taken the tube to defend himself, and yet he swung violently with it now, instinctively, grabbing at the chance to achieve a surprise attack before Phil Irish could launch himself at Henry. But his swing was low, aimed towards Phil Irish's ribs, and the man raised his left arm as though seeking to accommodate Henry rather than parry the blow. The tubing struck the Irishman along the left side with a cracking, smacking sound and Phil Irish staggered, went down with a soundless roaring and knelt there, leaning forward, his eyes glaring madly at Henry and his mouth open and shocked.

Henry too was shocked. For vital seconds he was unable to move. His fingers were nerveless, his breath tearing in his chest. Only when he saw Phil Irish begin to rise to his feet did he turn to run, and then it was too late. There was nowhere to run to; the roof ended only feet away and if he started to climb down the scaffolding Phil Irish would reach him in seconds, hurl him from the top. Henry backed away, raising the tube again as Phil Irish came up on his feet, swaying, his eyes hot with anger and his left arm curved in against his damaged ribs.

'*You little bastard!*'

The words came hissing out like venom from a snake. Henry backed away and was brought up short when his heel struck the base of the chimney stack. He dared not look around, for Phil Irish's eyes were fixed on his and the man was moving forward, lurching slightly.

'Stay away,' Henry shouted. 'Stay away or I'll hit you again!'

The big Irishman hesitated only a second, his eyes clouding as a sliver of pain darted through his rib cage, and then he lurched forward angrily as Henry swung the tube again. It came whistling through the air viciously, but Phil Irish was expecting it this time and he slipped sideways, snarling with pain as he did so, for the tube to clatter harmlessly past him against the ground. The shock sent a jarring pain up Henry's arm but he had no time to worry about that; the force of his swing had caught him off balance and Phil Irish was closing with him. Desperately he tried to bring the tube back in a wild defensive arc, but the Irishman was too quick for him. He was inside the swing, grabbing at Henry's arm, and next moment, with a swift, violent jerk, he had pulled Henry forward, completely off balance, and the tube dropped to the ground as Phil chopped at Henry's arm. Henry came on under the force of the Irishman's dragging hand, over the outstretched foot, and went sprawling down on the concrete, taking a strip of skin off his elbow and landing painfully on one shoulder. He turned, tried to scramble away, but Phil Irish was too quick for him. He stood there just two feet from Henry, half crouching, one arm still curved against his ribs, the other outstretched, fingers curling, a blaze of anger in his eyes. Henry looked down and saw the boots, the steel-capped boots, and one came forward, ready to kick him, ready to slam the breath out of his chest.

He looked up into Phil Irish's face and something in the desperation of his eyes must have given the Irishman pause. They stared at each other, like two crazed animals in whom the madness was suddenly dying. Perhaps Phil Irish was seeing Henry again, whereas a moment ago he had seen only an assailant; perhaps the puzzlement that was beginning to grow in his eyes had overcome the rage. Whatever it was he stopped coming forward and stood glaring at Henry, seemingly nonplussed.

Until the voice came from behind and above him, harsh, strident, razor-edged with hate.

'O'Hara! Are you looking for me?'

Phil Irish spun around, stepping sideways as he did so, and Henry was able to see past him, up to the catwalk and the girders some fifteen feet above their heads. Geordie Banion stood there, tall, spiderish, his greasy flat cap pulled forward over his eyes, his dark jacket flapping as the wind picked at it, lifted it against his back. He stood there in a curiously familiar stance, splayfooted, almost unsure of himself in a way Henry had never seen him on the girders. The familiarity was not of the heights; Banion looked different somehow to Henry, different and yet the same.

But the sameness was like an old, faded brown photograph, an image Henry had seen and not recognized, and at a distance, and with anxiety clouding his eyes, Henry was looking into a past that was recent for him, but long years ago for others. Banion stood there like a ghost, with his grey ravaged face and his hopeless mouth, and Phil Irish straightened slowly, staring up at him. Slowly he raised his fist, clenched not to strike Henry, but to smash into Geordie Banion if only he could reach him.

'I come to have it out with you, Banion!'

'I know,' Banion said, and his voice had changed, taken on almost a dreamlike quality. 'If you hadn't come...'

He did not finish the words, for Phil Irish almost screamed at him in a desperate, furious rage.

'What the bloody hell did you *do* it for? Why the hell couldn't you leave her alone?'

Banion shook his head slowly, a long, slow negative that was without reason. He stared down as Phil Irish almost ran forward, grabbing with both hands at the scaffolding, swinging out on to the poles and climbing rapidly, forgetful of his damaged ribs, driven on by a hate and anger that Henry could barely comprehend. Banion stood still, feet braced on the catwalk, arms dangling loosely at his side, and the wind rose as Phil Irish reached the catwalk, lifting his dark hair until it seemed to stand up horrendously. Henry watched the two men as they stood there, six feet separating them, and he heard Phil Irish shouting in a manic rage.

'For the first time in my life, Banion, I was ready

to run away from a fight! You know that, you bastard? I was ready to turn tail and get the hell out of it! Why the hell couldn't you leave it at that?'

'No.' The reply came in a measured tone and then, almost as though the wind took it and threw it skywards, it came again in a vast shout that more than matched Phil Irish's own. '*No!* I'd never have let her go off with you! Can't you see that? Never. Not you, nor anyone! *Never!*'

For a moment Phil Irish was quiet. He stood there glaring at the Tynesider, and almost unconsciously his hand crept up to caress the ribs that Henry had struck with the scaffolding pole. When he spoke his voice had dropped, and a wondering tone had entered it.

'I didn't know,' he said, 'I couldn't understand what the hell was going on. For a long time I thought you was just trying to get to grips with us as a gang; then I thought you'd got a sniff of Tommy Bighead's fiddle, and was putting the screws on us because you was frustrated, unable to find out where we was hiding the materials, how we was getting them off the site, who was organizing the whole job. Then I began to realize that it couldn't be that; began to guess there was something personal in it all, like. That day when you said I hadn't worked the overtime shift proper. That was when I began to get the message. You was so *sure* I hadn't, so I guessed you must have seen me down the town. But even then, I didn't understand.'

'You thick, horny Mick!'

Geordie Banion's face seemed even greyer and he was beginning to sway slightly, like a cobra about to strike at its enemy. Phil Irish shook his head in wonder. 'I should have seen it before, but I just never got the picture. I was too damned slow ... and I didn't know enough, that was it. You was needlin' me all the time but I never connected it with Helen!'

Banion stepped forward convulsively at the sound of her name and Phil Irish's hands came up, fingers curling slightly. 'Come on, you bastard, let's settle it then. Not by knockin' women about, but man to man!'

Banion leaned forward, his thin, wiry frame tense as a coiled spring. 'You think I *wanted* to hammer her, you stupid Mick?' he almost screamed. 'You think I went there to knock her about? You just don't understand! All I wanted to do was to try to make her see sense. I didn't want her to throw herself away on a clown like you, and I didn't want her to play around with youngsters like that kid down there! I wanted to explain to her, persuade her, but she got hysterical, started screaming at me. She was beside herself, and I slapped her.'

'*You fractured her bloody skull, man,* don't you realize that? After I got back from the site this morning, after I'd given in my notice, made some calls about a job in Cardiff; it was to find the place in a shambles and blood everywhere. I ran out to get to a phone but it was out of bloody order; I went back and the neighbours were already there, and I watched when the ambulance came and I phoned the hospital and they told me, and I came back to the site and hid in Twll-Mawr because I knew you'd damned well done it, I *knew* it!'

Banion clenched his fist and shook it with a repressed violence. 'It would never have been necessary if I'd got you the first time!'

The wind moaned around the chimney stack and Henry rose slowly to his feet. His eyes were riveted on the two men standing above his head. They stood there in silence, Geordie Banion leaning forward slightly from the hips, as though counterbalancing the force of the wind; Phil Irish, his whole body rigid, shaken.

'The *first* time?' he said. Geordie Banion made no reply and Henry walked forward slowly, quietly, until he stood just below the catwalk, staring up at the two above. 'The *first* time?' Phil Irish repeated stupidly and then, as his slow wits grasped the implication of Banion's words, his head came up. 'You tried to get me before ... *before* now? My God, *it was you killed Tommy Bighead!*'

Henry had got there before him. The pieces in the jigsaw were fitting into place. Geordie Banion had overheard the quarrel between Phil and Tommy Bighead – he had admitted as much to Gryfydd Morgan. What he had not told Morgan was that, knowing Phil Irish was to meet the encephalitic little man in the shed, he had climbed up above on the girders, climbed up to the deserted roof, where the breeze blocks and the joists lay, and he had looked down and played God.

'It wasn't Tommy Bighead I was after,' Banion said in a cold, even tone. 'I'd guessed about your fiddles, and the way things went on that morning you made it pretty obvious to everyone, you pack of fools, that something was up. It was you I was

224

after, O'Hara, and when I looked down and saw the shed door open I thought you'd be in there–'

'But Tommy had gone in first, and I was late! Hell's flames, Banion, you just didn't *care* who was in that shed!'

'Not as long as you were in there!'

'But for God's sake–'

'You don't understand, O'Hara, and you'll never understand. If you were capable of understanding even one tenth of it maybe I'd have left you and her alone, but you're nothing but a great, stupid, horny Mick, and I couldn't let her waste her life on you! You were no better – worse, in many ways – than that Rhayader crook! When I heard she had gone to work there, when I saw the way he was pestering her – because I watched, O'Hara, I've always watched – I tried to get back at him, warn him. I smashed his neon signs, I broke his windows, I even went into the club and vandalized the place. There was nothing else I could do, and besides, the thing wasn't serious – he never took her out, never went to her home. But I knew he wanted her, and I tried to make him pay, a little at least, for that lust! But you were different. You'd entered her life, got into her bed, damn you, and you *had* to pay! And that was my chance...'

Henry stood listening below them, rigid with shock. He could feel again the deathly passing of the joist, whirling through the air, and hear the slight sound it made as it fell. He could feel again the rain on his face, and see in his mind's eye the group of men on the ground, tearing at the shattered shed as Henry approached. He remembered how Banion had recoiled when he saw the corpse of Tommy Bighead, and he knew now it had not been shock at finding a dead man in the ruins, but shock that the dead man was Tommy Bighead. Banion had been above Henry, on the roof; agile on the girders and scaffolding he had swarmed down to the ground long before Henry could get there; and he had been on hand with the other arrivals to tear away at the timbers and the corrugated roof, to find Tommy Bighead, dead.

'You'll never appreciate how it is and how it's been,' Banion was saying, and his words had become reedy in the wind, insubstantial, complaining. 'She was in the gutter when I found her in Cardiff, and I loved her, and took her north and there was a good year, and then she changed. It was as though I couldn't give her enough; she was so dissatisfied. She wanted to be out, dancing, going to pubs, but she was *mine*, and I saw the way men looked at her! And she started to cheat on me, I was sure of it, but she was so bloody clever, I never caught her, I tried but I never caught her, and she was laughing at me!'

'You're the bloody fool, Banion!' Phil Irish shouted at him. 'You should have seen the way it was – you were obsessed, man!'

'I *married* her–'

'And it still wasn't enough, was it? She told me soon after I met her, told me all about *you!*' Phil Irish shouted. 'She told me about the man she lived with and married and was terrified by, in the end, so that she had to run away, get away from his obsessive jealousy. But she didn't tell me it was Geordie Banion, and she didn't tell me her

226

husband was here in Margam, or, by damn, I'd have sorted this out a long time ago! I didn't find out until last Saturday when we quarrelled, when all the hints and the questions and the situations finally got through my thick skull and I saw what it was all about, all the needling, and the fear. She was fed up running away, and she was looking for some sort of security – bloody hell, she even turned to that kid down there until I broke it up, knowing damn well that if you'd known she was turning to him you'd have clobbered Henry Jones as well!'

Henry shivered suddenly. Images were clicking through his brain like a shadowy film – a faded, badly-lit old photograph of a couple, just married; a man standing across the street, watching him curiously as he stumbled out, humiliated after Phil Irish's rough handling of him in Helen's flat. In both cases it had been Geordie Banion; and Phil's rage had been directed not towards Henry as such but towards Helen, for exposing Henry thoughtlessly to the danger of Geordie Banion's committed hate.

'...but I should have left well alone,' Phil Irish was shouting. 'I should have got the hell out of there, but I couldn't, she was so damn scared. So I agreed to take her away, make one last try at getting her hid from you, even if it meant getting more involved with her than I wanted to. My gut told me I ought to come and have it out with you, smash your face in. But for the first time I thought it out and decided to walk away. And I would have, too; I came up to the site, gave in my notice – and then found you'd gone into her flat as soon as I left, and almost killed her!'

'She wouldn't listen to me!' Banion's reedy voice rose almost to a scream above the rising wind. 'I pleaded with her – I've ruined my life too, you know that, following her from town to town! There was no peace, I had to be near her, I knew she'd come back to me one day, there'd be a time when she needed me, and I begged her – and then she lifted something and threw it at me, screamed at me, and everything boiled up–'

'*You bastard!*' Phil Irish snarled, and leaped forward with one hand reaching for Banion's throat.

If both men had been fit it could have been over within seconds, for Phil Irish, though no taller than Geordie Banion, was younger, stronger, thicker, more powerful. Banion was all steel and whipcord but he would have been no match for the younger man. Even so, as they stood locked together on the catwalk, almost motionless, there was no apparent advantage to Phil Irish, and Henry knew why. When Henry had struck him with the scaffolding tube he would have cracked a rib at least, and now, as Phil Irish strained at Geordie Banion's throat, every breath he took would be an agonized one, knives of pain slicing up through his chest. He had hate and a vengeful violence boiling in his veins, but it was matched by Banion's obsessive fury, and what Banion lacked in strength and power he could make up, for a few moments, in commitment. The pain evened out the rest; Henry could see Phil Irish's mouth open in agony as he strained at Geordie Banion's throat, and the Tynesider's wiry hands grappled with his wrists. Banion's body seemed

228

locked against the Irishman's and his hands were dragging at the grasping fingers, trying to tear them free, force them sideways. Both men were gasping, struggling now, forcing each other against the side of the catwalk, and Henry came to life at last. He put one hand up on the scaffolding, began to clamber up towards the men above him, and he looked down and he could see Morris Weasel's office and the police cars and the tiny figures of men clustering, staring upwards to the two men on the catwalk.

Henry climbed up, faster than he had ever managed to climb since he had come to the site. He was not clear *why* he climbed; he was vague as to what he hoped to achieve by getting up to the two men, but he felt he had to do something, commit himself in some way, if only because he had known Tommy Bighead and Helen Swain, and because he had made a bad mistake about Phil Irish, and injured him in the process.

Henry reached the catwalk. Phil and Geordie Banion were still locked together, struggling silently, but they had moved to the far end of the catwalk and their feet stamped and kicked against the metal, made the tubing ring and clang as they fought for supremacy. Their faces were twisted, and there was a line of spittle along Banion's mouth while the breath wheezed from Phil Irish's agonized chest in a manner that recalled for Henry the long painful walks Granda suffered up the hill to home. With one hand clinging to the scaffolding, Henry walked along the catwalk towards the antagonists, and he saw Geordie Banion's eyes flicker up, catch sight of him, and it was as though the Tynesider saw in Henry another assailant, for a wild panic came into his eyes and he drew on reserves of strength, broke Phil Irish's hold, and sent him staggering with a violent blow on the chest. Phil lurched back, half falling and colliding with Henry, and there was one long moment when Banion stood there, staring fixedly at them both. Then he turned and ran along the catwalk.

For more than two months Henry had seen Geordie Banion on the girders. He had seen him and marvelled at his agility as he moved swiftly across scaffolding and concrete ledges and steel girders, sure-footed as a mountain goat. There had been a time when Henry thought it would never have been possible for Geordie Banion ever to display a lack of confidence on the heights, but that had been before today, and now suddenly everything was changed. Perhaps it was a reflection of events; perhaps, in beating Helen Swain, Banion had reached a crisis point in his life that meant nothing would ever be the same again. But as he turned and scrambled away he was no longer the same man. His movements were uncoordinated, his step broken, almost puppet-like in its jerkiness and uncertainty. His arms seemed to flap helplessly as he ran, and his whole body seemed to tremble as he lurched and staggered, drunk with the height, panicked, lost and desperate. He reached the end of the catwalk and tried to duck under the girder that barred entry to the scaffolding pinned into the breeze blocks beyond. He struck his forehead against the girder and the force of the blow made him stagger. He reached up, grabbed the scaffolding with his left hand and hauled himself up, but his movement was slow and painful. He glared back towards Henry and his face was deathly white, his eyes black holes in his face, expressionless, staring. He pulled himself up on to the scaffolding and he was twenty feet away from them as Phil Irish stood up. Phil shouted unintelligibly, and the sound bounced off the breeze blocks and made Banion's body jerk. He drew up his legs, attempted to stand, and his boot slipped; he lost balance, and then he was hanging by both hands, his body loose, his head turned as he stared back towards Henry and Phil Irish.

It was a moment Henry knew he would remember all his life. Geordie Banion was suspended from the scaffolding with his back to the catwalk. Only three feet separated him from the catwalk itself, three feet behind and below him. Yet he made no attempt to stretch out, take his weight on one foot. Instead, he just hung there and stared at Henry.

Yet he saw nothing. The images were all inside his head and formed part of a dream that had never really existed. They might have been soft images, ideas and pictures such as everyone kept within the private recesses of his mind. They had nothing to do with reality; they were rooted in the past. And when his eyes cleared after a moment, and the reality became apparent and the present was with him, Geordie Banion looked at Henry and Phil Irish and he let go.

It was possible he broke his back within the first twenty feet of his fall, for when he deliberately released his grip on the scaffolding he dropped down against the guard rail of the concrete roof below and Henry heard a horrible snapping sound. There was the chance that Banion might have stopped even then, grabbed at the edge of the roof, had he wanted to, or been able to, but the desire was lacking. He made no cry, made no sound. In a moment he was gone and all Henry could remember was the hurt in the man's eyes when the truth had come rushing in on him, drowning the dreams of the past and all those forlorn, lost hopes for a future that had never really existed.

'What the hell did he do that for?' Phil Irish muttered in a shocked, awed voice.

4

Henry tried to explain it to Brenda, nevertheless, at the weekend. He made an attempt to explain to her how it must have been with Geordie Banion. A cold, shy man who had loved a woman so deeply and so possessively that she had become the focus for an existence that became unbearable. To live with her was not enough; to marry her was not enough. She had been all he wanted and yet she had been too much for him. He had never been able to accept that she had an existence of her own and the obsession had come to dominate his life and destroy whatever feeling she had for him. And when she had fled from him he could not let her go; he had followed her, from Hartlepool to Liverpool, from the North

232

back to Wales. At first he would have attempted to force her to return to him, but later, at Margam, he had stayed in the background, near her, watching her, always watching.

Helen Swain had tried to shut him out of her life and had succeeded to a large extent. She knew he was working at Margam to be near her; she knew that he watched her from a distance. She must have suspected that the vandalism at The Brick Wall might have been Geordie Banion's work, but she had tried to think otherwise, shut him out of her mind. And Banion had gradually worked himself up into an obsessive rage as he watched her, saw her take Phil Irish as a lover. At first he had not known how to deal with the situation and it had spilled over into an open dislike of the Irishman on the site. But it had finally exploded and Tommy Bighead had died.

'But he hadn't intended killing Tommy,' Henry told Brenda. 'It was Phil he was after, and Tommy's death was a mistake, really. I think he was up there, high, and he saw the shed door open and it was just like playing God, having power to right what he saw as a wrong done to him, you know?'

'Never mind, is it,' Brenda replied with a sigh. 'Well away from them all up at that place, you are.'

But in a sense Henry would never be away from them all at North Margam. The weeks he had spent on that building site had been important to him. They had been lost weeks, in one sense; a time when he had drifted, lost his way, made a gesture as though gestures were important, even

233

though you didn't know what you were trying to prove. But if they had been lost weeks, they had been weeks when he had gradually come to realize that the things held important by an old man, who had lived most of his life, could also be important to a woman who had seen more than her share of unhappiness. For Helen Swain and Granda had had that much in common: they had both seen their distant banners and reached for them. Granda had been lucky – he had held his in his hands. Helen Swain had found that her goal was unattainable, for it had been nothing but pain. And yet she had still subscribed to the principle.

Even Geordie Banion had seen his banner; and when it was finally lost to him there was nothing left to live for. This was what Henry haltingly tried to explain to Brenda. It was what he had read in Geordie Banion's eyes in that moment before the Tynesider gave up his grip on the scaffolding and on life. He had seen himself and his obsession in clear, clinical terms for the first time; he had realized how his need for Helen Swain would never be assuaged and yet had come to dominate his life; and in that moment he had known he no longer wanted to hold on to that life. He could never be to Helen what she was to him, and so there was nothing left to live for.

Henry could think back to them all now and see how they had all carved out for themselves a role in life, in a way Henry Jones had not. Gryfydd Morgan wanted to be as successful a policeman as he had been a front row forward and his objective was to reach the pinnacle by playing the same basic rules; Arfon Rhayader wanted to be a

234

millionaire and maybe would be one day, once he had served the term of imprisonment that was now sure to come his way; for Morris Weasel and Tonto Thomas the aims were smaller, for they were smaller men – a regular job and a fiddle on the side, and now, for a while, they would lose both as a result of Morgan's exposure of the thefts at North Margam building site. In a sense, only Jayo Davies had won: all he wanted was a peaceful existence, an uncomplicated life where people would not bother him. He had co-operated with Morgan and so charges would probably not be preferred. A few shifts each week, a contemplation of the sky, on his back in the dunes, it was a simple enough objective for a man.

'It's Phil Irish and Helen Swain I wonder about,' Henry said to Brenda. 'Phil will have to face charges over the fiddling, but I think Morgan will be more than happy to have his testimony over the murder of Tommy Bighead, and he should get off pretty lightly. And Helen Swain will be out of hospital in a week or so. But the thing is, will she and Phil get together? I mean, in a sense Phil *committed* himself to her when he came back that night and agreed to take her away, rather than have things out with Banion. Yet it was a reluctant committal, and I wonder whether it will be the same now that the pressure has gone with Banion dead. Maybe Helen Swain will find that what she wants – to settle down with a man like Phil – is still unattainable. Sad, really, isn't it?'

'I don't know about that,' Brenda said some- what testily. 'Don't know why you keep on about it all. Better to put all that nasty business behind you, it is. We got our own future to settle, haven't we?'

And that evening they settled it. Brenda sat at one side of the table and Granda was in his usual easy chair and Nan was making a cup of tea, like always. And the conversation rolled endlessly on, the basic facts in issue being rolled up like the fruit in a Christmas cake, larded around by a doughy mass of anecdotes, and names, and events; it was never enough to mention who could help Henry Jones in his future career, it was necessary to explain that person's antecedents and who they had married and what they had died of and how many other children and aunts and cousins they had had in their time. And as the conversation went on Henry began to realize for the first time that it wasn't really a buying and selling at all, it wasn't a market place as he had said to Helen Swain. Rather, it was one vast system of barter, where a man gave himself to a community and that community gave itself to him. In one sense the individual became lost in the whole; in another, he triumphed above the mass, for he could point to what the whole had given to him, merely for *being*. The valley looked after its sons, for the sons *were* the valley.

'Aye, all right,' he said suddenly, and Brenda and Granda looked at him in surprise. When he said no more they returned to their conversation about him and his future in the bank, and the number of councillors they could approach to assure his future. Henry was hardly listening. It was some sort of banner, at least – marriage with Brenda and manager of the bank, maybe in Treorchy. Everyone ought to have a distant banner to aim for; Granda and Helen and all the others were right.

And for the time being, this one would do, he'd commit himself to it – and with a little help from his friends, he'd reach it. And more than that, as he looked around and saw Nan bustling across with the tea and Brenda and Granda talking excitedly together about the future, he realized *they* had not looked so happy for a long, long time.

So there was that to be said for it, at least.

The publishers hope that this book has given you enjoyable reading. Large Print Books are especially designed to be as easy to see and hold as possible. If you wish a complete list of our books please ask at your local library or write directly to:

Magna Large Print Books
Magna House, Long Preston,
Skipton, North Yorkshire.
BD23 4ND

This Large Print Book for the partially sighted, who cannot read normal print, is published under the auspices of

THE ULVERSCROFT FOUNDATION

THE ULVERSCROFT FOUNDATION

... we hope that you have enjoyed this Large Print Book. Please think for a moment about those people who have worse eyesight problems than you ... and are unable to even read or enjoy Large Print, without great difficulty.

You can help them by sending a donation, large or small to:

**The Ulverscroft Foundation,
1, The Green, Bradgate Road,
Anstey, Leicestershire, LE7 7FU,
England.**
or request a copy of our brochure for more details.

The Foundation will use all your help to assist those people who are handicapped by various sight problems and need special attention.

Thank you very much for your help.